### *"Are you saying you can't resist me?" Michael asked.*

"Of course not," Suzanne snapped. "It's just—"

"There are two doors between us. You can shove a chair under the knob if you think your charm is so fatal that my self-control will fail."

She thought of hot, deep kisses and his hard male body pressing into hers—but she reminded herself that she'd just seen a side of him she hadn't known. He'd just demonstrated how unsuitable she'd always known they were.

This man had women aplenty only too happy to fall into his arms.

"Fine. But knock before you enter the dressing room, and I'll do the same."

He nodded. "I'll be downstairs whenever you're ready to leave. Look around all you want. I have no secrets."

She watched him go, mouth agape at the blatant falsehood. Maybe he really believed that, but she knew she'd never met a more complicated or mystifying man in her life.

# THE **COLTONS**

*Meet the Coltons—
a California dynasty with a legacy
of privilege and power.*

**Michael Longstreet:** *Prosperino's golden boy.* He'd grown up with his wealthy parents granting his every wish. But now they have a wish of their own—for him to find a bride ASAP....

**Suzanne Jorgenson:** *Tireless social worker.* Only one man can get under her skin, and now a small child's welfare depends on her *marrying* him!

**Bobby Roper:** *Lost-and-found child.* Now that his adoptive parent can no longer care for him, he's about to be reunited with the one woman who has never stopped loving him.

**Rafe James:** *The very private P.I.* He has some ideas about who might be responsible for the town's current crisis—he just doesn't know how *personally* involved he's about to become....

# SWEET CHILD
# OF MINE

## Jean Brashear

Published by Silhouette Books
**America's Publisher of Contemporary Romance**

Special thanks and acknowledgment are given
to Jean Brashear for her contribution
to THE COLTONS series.

**SILHOUETTE BOOKS**

ISBN 0-373-21744-7

SWEET CHILD OF MINE

Visit Silhouette at www.eHarlequin.com

**Printed in U.S.A.**

# About the Author

**JEAN BRASHEAR**

A Texan to her toes, award-winning author
Jean Brashear still couldn't help falling in love
with Northern California from the moment she
saw it, so the invitation to be part of a series set
there was thrilling. An avid reader from childhood,
she has been in love with romance almost as long
as she's been in love with books. She considers
Silhouette a wonderful fairy godmother for giving
her the chance to share that love with readers, as
the joy of writing stories is one that never pales.
She welcomes mail from readers at P.O. Box 40012,
Georgetown, TX 78628 or via the Silhouette Web site
at www.eHarlequin.com.

To my beloved brother Buddy and his lovely Liz,
and to their sweet Jackie, Jimmy, Justin, Joey
and Jenny, with great affection and heartfelt thanks
for cheering me on.

# One

"**M**ichael, your father just wants to know that you'll have someone of your own. We worry about you being alone. He needs the peace of mind."

"I'm not alone, Mom. I have plenty of friends." Michael Longstreet leaned back in his chair, boots propped up on the desk, and squeezed his eyes shut. Telephone cradled on one shoulder, he stared out his law office window. The quiet of Prosperino's Main Street in early February was something he normally looked forward to, but this year was anything but normal.

His town was in trouble. His father's heart was giving out. His mother, usually so relentless in her need to meddle in his life, had turned frail overnight.

"And I had someone," he continued to make his case. "I had Elaine."

"I know." Her voice fell. "I can't help thinking that if we'd given our blessing to your marriage, she and the baby would still be alive."

*No, Mom. That's not on your shoulders. That blame is all mine.* "Mom, don't—"

"It's just that he worries about you."

"I know." It was an old record, the grooves worn thin. "But there's no reason to worry. My life is fine. I've got my work and my duties as mayor—" He glanced at his watch and shoved to his feet. Rory Sinclair, the FBI expert investigating the contamination of the Hopechest Ranch well, had asked for a meeting that would begin in half an hour.

"Mom, I've got to go. I'm sorry. There's a meeting about Hopechest. I'll stop by and see Dad in the morning, all right?"

"Michael, will the town's water be all right?" She sounded old, all of a sudden. Tremulous in a way that worried him.

"Sure it will," he said, with a confidence he couldn't back up with facts. It was his main task lately, projecting assurance so that people wouldn't panic. "The FBI is on the case and they're getting close, they tell me. We'll know soon what made so many people sick." He stood up, ran his fingers through his hair and wondered when he'd ever get a good night's sleep again. "Listen, Mom, I've got to go now, but don't you worry. I can't magically produce a wife to make Dad happy, but I'll talk to him again, make sure he sees that I'm just fine. I'll figure out a way to ease his mind." And he would, just as he'd always done his duty by his family.

With one notable exception.

He listened to his mother for another few moments, made sure that she was steadier before he said goodbye. Then he glanced at his watch again, grabbed his jacket and strode out the door.

Mayor Longstreet was on the job.

Something was wrong with Suzanne Jorgenson.

That evening Michael frowned, watching the slender, dark-haired social worker standing so quietly at the podium. The emergency city council meeting was jammed with anxious citizens, all talking at once.

A voice lifted above the rest. "Michael, how do we know this DM—uh—"

"DMBE," he supplied. He'd only heard of the substance an hour ago himself.

"Whatever," the man in the second row shouted. "My wife's pregnant and we've got three other kids. What makes you think the contaminated water is only at Hopechest Ranch?"

Michael leaned closer to his microphone, praying for the right words. The air was thick with fear. A full-blown panic wasn't far off.

"The only people who've gotten sick have been

either kids who live at Hopechest or townspeople who work there.''

''Why would anybody want to poison a ranch full of kids?'' someone asked.

''Those kids are troublemakers. Even their parents don't want them,'' said a disgruntled voice.

Finally Michael saw a spark in Suzanne's deep violet eyes. Her long hair swung as she turned quickly to pin the speaker with a glare. ''Just because it's been forty years since you had kids around, Homer Wentworth, doesn't mean you have no responsibility to help those less fortunate.''

Michael tried not to gloat. Old Wentworth wanted to raise the drawbridge around his property and ignore the rest of the world—until his taxes were impacted.

He'd picked the wrong person to spar with. Suzanne Jorgenson was passionate about one thing beyond anything else: troubled children. In the months since she'd come to Prosperino, he'd seen the raven-haired beauty standing at the podium in city council chambers many times—usually chewing him out for all the shortcomings of the city he ran, full of suggestions for ways to better the lives of Prosperino's neglected children. She would work herself into the ground to give them the love and support she firmly believed should be every child's God-given right.

Michael was accustomed to the crackle in the air from her boundless well of energy, her St. George-against-the-dragon flair. He would even admit to enjoying baiting her simply to see the sparks flare from those bottomless eyes. There was very little that was restful about the social worker whose primary responsibility was the unwed mothers at Emily's House. Hopechest Ranch had not been the same since her arrival a year ago.

But no one was peaceful in Prosperino now—not with the threat of a contaminated water supply hanging over them. And tonight was a night for pulling together, not butting heads.

He tapped his gavel for order and leaned toward his microphone. "Homer, I want to assure you and all the citizens of Prosperino that every possible avenue is being explored to protect the safety of the citizens. The city wells are being monitored—"

"Some folks think it's best to leave town, Mayor." This from an elderly lady near the back.

"That's up to the individual, of course. For myself, I'll be staying here. I have every faith that we'll soon know how DMBE got into the well at Hopechest. In the meantime, we have experts standing by, generously paid for by Joe Colton, who are working night and day on a solution to removing the substance from the water, should it reach the town's water supply."

There was a smattering of applause for the town's leading citizen, Joe Colton, and his wife, Meredith. The dark-haired older man nodded his head in acknowledgment.

Michael waited for the applause to fade. "Our next

concern is what to do with the children at Hopechest who haven't fallen ill. Blake, could you tell us more about what you need?''

Blake Fallon, director of Hopechest Ranch, was standing beside Suzanne and nodded. ''We're looking for as many as thirty homes in which to place one or two of the kids. We'd prefer them to not stay at the ranch, even with water being trucked in, until we can be sure it won't happen again.'' His voice was calm as always. A less steady man would never have lasted at Hopechest.

''Blake,'' Joe Colton called as he stood up, tall and distinguished. ''Meredith and I have a solution we'd like to offer. We have plenty of room on the ranch for the kids who need a place to stay. That way they wouldn't have to be split up.''

Suzanne stirred. ''Mr. Colton, the girls at Emily's House need special diets, along with transportation for regular doctor's visits. Are you sure about this?''

Joe nodded. ''Hopechest Ranch is our baby.'' He smiled fondly at the wife he'd almost lost. ''This feels right to us. The staff at Hopechest can set up the usual routines for however long our quarters are needed. We'll do everything possible to meet the needs of these very deserving children.''

Michael wanted to chuckle when some of Suzanne's normal sass revealed itself in the triumphant look she shot back at Homer Wentworth.

That was more like it.

Blake Fallon smiled broadly. "Thanks, Joe. We'll do everything in our power to make this as easy on you and Meredith as possible. Won't we, Suzanne?"

The long fall of her straight black hair shimmered on her shoulders as Suzanne nodded vigorously. "Absolutely."

"All right," Michael said. "The city secretary will be placing a daily update on the city's Web site, and for those of you who insist on pretending the Internet doesn't exist—" he grinned good-naturedly "—a printed memo will be posted on the bulletin board outside city offices."

He scanned the room and waited for total silence to fall. "My father is very ill and I have no intention of moving him out of Prosperino, nor do I plan to leave myself. That's how sure I am that it will all work out. I want every citizen of this town to know that all possible resources are being tapped to ensure their safety, and I have every faith that we will succeed. You all know where my office is—hell, most of you wind up on my front porch at one time or another." He grinned as laughter traveled around the room.

"I'm not going anywhere and I'm available whenever you have a question, all right? We're in this together, and I won't rest until we get this puzzle solved. Now, anybody have another question?" He waited patiently, but no one spoke up.

"All right, then. This meeting is adjourned." He

brought the gavel down and rose, pulling his battered leather jacket from the chair behind him. Within seconds, people surrounded him, all wanting answers he didn't have, but he would do his best to soothe them, to instill confidence in the government he headed. That was his job as mayor and a duty he held sacred. This town was his responsibility, just as were his dying father and his frightened mother.

Michael Longstreet had had one spectacular failure as a young husband and father and it had cost him the family he should have saved.

Never again would someone in his care suffer.

"Let's go talk to Joe and see how soon he can take the kids," Blake Fallon said.

Suzanne flicked a glance toward the dais where Michael Longstreet held court. With her accursed sensitivity to the emotional temperature of her surroundings, Suzanne felt the anxiety of the crowd pummel her already battered nerves, but she could feel the lowering of the tension around her.

Thanks to Mr. Mayor's glib tongue.

"Suz?" Blake broke in. "Did you hear what I asked?"

"Oh—yes. Sure. Let's go."

That was a cheap shot, calling him glib. Yes, Michael Longstreet had the devil's own silver tongue. He could probably call the birds down from the trees. He'd certainly gotten the upper hand often enough when she'd tangled with him. She glanced back toward the dais and saw his shaggy, sun-streaked brown hair as he towered above most of his constituents. In his usual jeans and boots, no one would guess he was a graduate of Yale and Georgetown Law School, smart, rich and, yes, too good-looking. When he could have been a partner in any Wall Street firm, why had he come back to Prosperino?

She didn't know and couldn't care. As she walked toward Joe and Meredith Colton, she could only be concerned about the kids of Hopechest Ranch. She had eight homeless pregnant girls at Emily's House. Despite the doctor's reassurances, they were still worried about the effects of DMBE on their babies.

Then there were the forty-eight kids at Hopechest Ranch right now, some of whom were at delicate stages in their emotional development. She'd have to find extra time to keep meeting with the kids, one on one, to monitor their emotional well-being.

A light touch on her arm brought her up short. "Suzanne, you look tired. This must be very hard on you and Blake," said Meredith Colton, gracious and elegant as always, her warm brown eyes filled with sympathy.

"The whole staff's pretty tired. No one's gotten much sleep since this thing started."

"But are you sure that's all that's wrong? You seem so—" Ever the soul of discretion, Meredith didn't continue.

As soon as she could get away, Suzanne was going to crawl in a hole somewhere and hide from the bombshell that had been dropped right into her dreams just as she was about to leave for the meeting tonight.

Joe Colton and Blake looked at her oddly, and Suzanne straightened. She would lick her wounds in private. "I'm just fine. It's the kids I'm worried about. Tell us how you want to work out the details of turning your beautiful home into an orphanage."

Joe and Meredith laughed and even Blake, exhausted and worried as he was, cracked a smile.

Suzanne shoved away the blues and concentrated on the children under her care.

"See you in the morning, Blake." Michael waved at his troubled friend. "Go get some sleep. It'll all be here tomorrow."

Blake shook his head. "Yeah. That's what I'm afraid of."

"We're going to lick this, buddy. Your friend Sinclair broke the case, and the FBI's now involved. The EPA guys are champing at the bit after Inspector O'Connell's death. We'll find out who and why and what we have to do. Joe's brought all his resources to bear, too."

"But what if—"

Michael knew exactly what Blake meant. He wouldn't be sleeping soundly at night until they knew for sure how the DMBE got into the Hopechest water and could be sure it hadn't traveled into the city's wells. But he'd learned long ago that lying awake didn't do anything but make you too tired to deal with tomorrow. "Tomorrow, Blake," he said firmly. "No more for you tonight." With a friendly push, he sent his friend toward his car. "Home. Sleep."

Blake saluted, got into his car and drove away.

Michael stood on Prosperino's Main Street and looked around him at the town where his childhood memories had been born. He thought of the son who'd never ride his bike on these streets, never climb a tree. He felt an echo of the old, gut-wrenching pain and looked up at the stars.

Not one parent in Prosperino is going to lose a child, I swear it. I will not rest until everyone here is safe again, no matter what it takes.

There was nothing he could do to safeguard the woman and child buried, along with his heart, a continent away. There was nothing he could do to make his father's long-damaged heart mend. Nor was there anything he could—or would—do to satisfy his father's dying wish for Michael to marry.

But he could expend every ounce of his determination and strength to keep the citizens of this town safe. Corny as it might sound, they were his responsibility. He had taken an oath to serve this town that was so much a part of him, of his family's heritage, and he would honor that oath.

Michael's senses registered the breeze through the trees, the muffled sounds of slow, small-town living. Suddenly he realized he hadn't eaten since breakfast. He was starving. His gaze lit on Ruby's Café, the heartbeat of Prosperino. He didn't feel like going home to an empty house tonight. Ruby's, it was. With quick strides, he headed down the block.

When he entered the café, quiet at this late hour, he was stopped at every occupied table or booth by people seeking reassurance. He did the best he could, though it had been a very long day and all he really wanted was some peace and quiet and food.

He spoke with the last group and traded handshakes all around, then headed for his favorite back booth.

But it was occupied—by the very woman he'd been worried about earlier.

Staring into a coffee cup, looking utterly lost, Suzanne Jorgenson seemed to gather what little light made it into that corner of the room. Sleek and straight, her black hair fell past her shoulders, veiling her face as she leaned forward, her head in her hands.

Suzanne was a good foot shorter than his own six four, but her will was so strong and her spirit so indomitable that she'd always seemed taller. Tonight she looked fragile and vulnerable, and it shocked Michael so much that he wasn't sure whether to go to her or retreat.

But he'd never been much for retreating.

"Mind if I join you?"

Her head jerked up, and he could see that she'd been crying. On her lovely face was a look of such despair that it didn't matter how tired he was. Instead of waiting for an answer she seemed too dazed to give, he sat down. "What's wrong?"

For a moment the old sparks flickered in those stunning violet eyes. "I don't recall inviting you to sit down, Mr. Mayor." But he heard the tremble in her voice.

"So sue me. What's wrong? The kids are going to be okay, I swear it. We've got lots of people working on this. The ranch isn't alone anymore."

"It isn't—" She stopped, but he could see temptation flicker.

He cocked his head. "Is there something about the ranch I need to know? Something you and Blake haven't told us?"

She shook her head slowly. "It's not the ranch. It's—" She glanced away. "Nothing. Not anything you need to worry about."

But she was worried, desperately so. He made his living reading people—in court, in depositions, in the confidences they shared with him. He also knew the value of silence. "I've got pretty broad shoulders and a willing ear to spare."

When her gaze flickered over him, measuring those shoulders, Michael felt an answering response, and the strength of it surprised him. Well, all right, it wasn't like he'd never looked at her as a woman. But most of the time she was a pain in the behind, always involved in some cause or other, always trying to push for the city to pitch in, always impatient with the pace of bureaucracy.

But he had noticed she was female. She was slender though definitely curved in all the right places. You couldn't look at her with those big violet eyes and those knockout legs and not know she was all woman. If she'd use that delectable mouth for something besides arguing with him over every line of the city budget as though the only important causes were hers—

He caught himself staring at that mouth and turned away quickly, calling out his order to Ruby.

"No date tonight, Mr. Mayor?" There it was, that tone she used, that snotty tone that made him—

She didn't want to talk about whatever it was that was making her cry, so she must be out to pick a fight.

He wasn't going to cooperate. "Nope. No date. Doesn't look too good for the head of the emergency management team to be playing while the Titanic sinks."

Her eyes went wide, and she shifted in the booth. "Oh God, the kids—"

He stopped her with one raised palm. "It was a joke, Jorgenson. All right, a lousy one, but I'm a little punchy. We've been putting in some long nights lately."

Suddenly her eyes softened. "Blake's exhausted."

"I'll bet you are, too. You've been at the hospital every day and all that driving back and forth to the ranch trying to keep the kids calm has to be wearing you out. You should be home asleep, you know. You won't do them any good if you wind up in a bed beside them."

She studied him for a long moment. "Careful, Longstreet. I might get the idea that you're a decent guy."

He shrugged and grinned. "I even have a mother who thinks I'm pretty terrific. Go figure." He watched her closely. He took one more stab, keeping his tone light. "So if it's not the ranch, is it some deep, dark secret that I can exploit the next time you're haranguing me at the council meeting?"

She made a halfhearted attempt to rise to the bait. "Can't help you there. Sorry."

The waitress walked up with his food, and Suzanne fell silent.

Michael didn't speak either but tucked into his meal, savoring the first bites of Ruby's meat loaf from heaven. After he'd satisfied the initial hunger pangs, he looked at Suzanne again, observing the slim fingers clutching the coffee cup until her knuckles turned white.

He went on impulse. "Give me a dollar."

Her head jerked up again. "What?"

"Give me a dollar." He spied the change beside

her cup and grabbed it. "Never mind. Thirty-seven cents will do."

"What are you doing?"

"You just hired me as your lawyer. Now I can't reveal to a soul anything you tell me. So spill it, Suzanne. Something's eating you up and you need to talk about it."

She stared at him as though he'd lost his mind.

Then the tears spilled over.

"I'm going to lose my son. For the second time."

# Two

"**Y**ou what?" Michael's deep green eyes widened. The shock of sun-streaked brown hair that always fell over his forehead bounced as his head reared up. "You have a son? Where is he?"

"He's in Sacramento with his father. Well, not his—" Yes, Jim Roper was Bobby's father, the only one he'd ever known. "He's with his father." She lapsed into silence.

She expected a volley of questions, but instead Michael waited her out.

She reached for the saltshaker on the table in front of him, sliding it around in aimless circles until she realized what she was doing and jerked her hand back, trapping it in her lap. "I—" She glanced up once, then down quickly, but he didn't look impatient. Instead he sat there, fork still, simply watching her with only concern in his eyes.

"Your food will get cold. Go ahead and eat," she said.

"My food can wait. Talk to me, Suzanne."

The gentle tone was something she'd never heard from him. They'd always been too busy striking sparks off each other, arguing vigorously in one meeting or another.

She realized that she'd never been alone with Michael Longstreet before. There was a stillness about the man that seeped beneath her skin, a patience that made her realize how much she needed to talk to someone.

"I had to give him up for adoption." She kept her eyes on her coffee cup. "I didn't want to, but it was the right thing to do. I was sixteen. I couldn't have cared for him the way he deserved." She couldn't risk a glance upward, couldn't bear seeing if his expression disapproved. No matter how often she'd told herself she'd done the right thing, it still hurt. She'd still wanted her baby back, sometimes so much she thought she couldn't last into the next breath.

Anyway, it was done. It was over—or it had been over. But not anymore.

"A few months ago I received a call from Jim Roper, the man who adopted my baby. Bobby—"

She looked up then and couldn't help a smile. "His name is Bobby. He'll be ten soon." And oh, how she wanted to celebrate his birthday with him. Wanted to bake him a cake with her own hands and blow up balloons and do all the things she'd wanted to do every March 28th of the last nine years.

"What happened to his biological father?" Michael asked.

She glanced away. "He didn't want a baby. His future was too bright, he said. Too much of his life ahead of him. He offered me money for an abortion and made it clear that he wanted nothing to do with a child he doubted was his own."

A low curse issued from Michael's throat, and she gathered the courage to look back. She saw his eyes darken with outrage, but on his face she saw more than that, a swirling of strong emotions she couldn't define. "I'd never been with anyone else. Fool that I was, I actually thought we were in love, this rich man's son and the daughter of a plumber." A rich man's son like the one who sat before her.

Michael didn't miss the accusation in her voice. If only she knew. He'd made the opposite choice from her rich boy and married the waitress his parents tried to buy off, knowing his parents would cut him off without a penny. Feeling righteous because he loved her so much.

His foolish pride had ultimately cost his wife and unborn baby their lives.

Michael jerked his dark thoughts back to the woman across the table. "He didn't deserve you. He wouldn't have made you happy."

Suddenly, her eyes filled with tears. "But I could have kept my baby—" She grasped her napkin in white-knuckled fingers and sniffed hard, forcing the tears back. "No, you're right. I know I did the best thing for Bobby, but—" Her hands fluttered from the table, palms up in helplessness.

"So now you fight like a tigress for other people's children."

The violet gaze shifted to his, the thick black lashes still shimmering with tears. The corners of her full mouth tilted slightly, and she nodded. "I guess so."

"So what's happened now, tonight?"

The faint smile vanished. She twisted the paper napkin through her fingers. "When Jim Roper contacted me, it was because Bobby had been wanting to meet his biological mother. His adoptive mother died five years ago, and Jim has been raising Bobby alone." Her face brightened in a way he'd never seen. "He's done a good job. Bobby's a bright, healthy, energetic boy who's very secure in the love he's been given."

Her gaze lifted to his. "I was so afraid to meet Bobby, even though Jim and I agreed to take it slow and not tell him yet that I was his mother. Give him time to get used to me, to decide if he liked me without all that pressure." Moisture glistened again, one slow tear trailing down her cheek. "He likes me, but I'm so afraid that he'll hate me when he knows." The napkin tore in her fingers. "And now it's too late."

Michael frowned. "Why?"

"Jim hasn't been feeling well. He finally went to the doctor last week and found out that he's got pancreatic cancer. He doesn't have long. He wants me to take Bobby."

"Don't you want to?"

Her head snapped up. "Of course I do, more than I've ever wanted anything in my life. But Jim's wife has a cousin named in his will as guardian if anything happens to Jim."

"So? He can change the will."

"He's afraid she'll contest it because I'm single and I don't have a long job history or much money. The cousin is married and is financially secure." She looked up at him, and he wasn't sure he'd ever seen such misery in his life. "I understand. I do. Jim doesn't have much to leave for Bobby, so he needs to be sure Bobby's in the best hands. It's just that—" Her voice broke, and he saw her shoulders shake. "I feel like I'm losing him all over again. Jim says he believes that I'd be the best mother, but he admits that the cousin would be good to Bobby and she's got all the things that I don't."

"Like a husband and solid financial footing?"

Her eyes sparked as she nodded. Her voice was fierce when she spoke. "But I have love, so much love. All the love he could ever want. And it's going to be so hard on him, anyway, losing Jim. He doesn't know this cousin, and he really likes me, I know he does. Jim says so, too, says he's never seen Bobby take to someone so quickly.

"Isn't this ridiculous?" she asked through a sheen of tears. "It sounds like a great soap opera plot, I'm sure."

Michael shook his head. "In your work and mine, we both see a lot of messy situations. Life is like that."

"Mine's not. Not usually."

"Want me to see if I could negotiate something? It's what I do for a living, after all."

She shook her head. "Jim is too sick. I'm worried about the strain on him. He's holding it together for Bobby right now, but I think it's sheer will. He needs a quick and easy solution, and the easiest thing is just to give in and not fight this. Maybe I'm being selfish, wanting Bobby back so badly."

Remembering how badly Elaine had wanted their baby, Michael shook his head. "You gave him up once, despite what you wanted. I don't think selfish applies."

She ran the fingers of one hand through the long, silky mane and tried to smile. "Jim said it was too bad I couldn't just order up a husband. He thinks he could get the cousin to back off if he's able to show her that I could give Bobby as much as she could."

She glanced up at Michael. "Know any likely candidates, Counselor? Since you're on retainer and all, I might as well get my money's worth." She strove for lightness, but in her eyes swam pure misery.

Michael thought about his conversation with his mother and almost laughed, except it wasn't funny. Just hours ago he'd been gnashing his teeth, wishing for a way to ease his father's last days but unable to stomach the hypocrisy of searching for a temporary wife.

He shook his head. Surely he couldn't seriously be considering the obvious option. He had the solution for both of them right in his hands, but—

He knew he couldn't rule it out. Fate was a quirky, ill-tempered witch, but every once in a while, she smiled your way. "What would you do with this husband if you found him?" He strove for a casual tone.

"I'd kiss his feet if he'd help me get my son."

"You only want a man long enough to get custody of your child, is that it?" He didn't know why that pricked at his temper. It was perfect. All he wanted was a way to make his dad happy for whatever time remained. He had no heart left to give a woman.

But Suzanne didn't look cynical. Just worn and sad. "My only concern has to be Bobby right now. But it doesn't matter, anyway. There's no candidate running around."

Michael took a quick glance out the window, wondering if he could really do this.

Then he looked back at the woman across from him, and the slope of defeat in her shoulders tugged at his conscience. He could help her out and make his dad happy at the same time. She didn't want more than he could give. All her love would go to her son. If he were the one dying and having to leave a son behind, he'd want that son to have a mother's love as fierce as Suzanne's.

"Maybe there is someone."

Her head jerked up. Her eyes narrowed. "That's not funny, Michael. Please...I don't feel like sparring now."

"I'm not sparring. And I'm not joking. Maybe I've got a solution for you."

Any hesitation he felt was doomed, once he saw the flare of intense joy in her eyes. Quickly, she banked it, holding herself stiffly as if afraid to trust his words. Her tone was guarded as she responded. "And what might that solution be?"

Here goes nothing. He felt a swift inner clench as he opened his mouth to speak.

"You could marry me."

Suzanne would have thought despair had dulled her capacity for shock, but obviously not. Dire as her situation was, she felt stunned laughter bubble up in her throat. "You're kidding, right?"

Eyes the color of moss by a mountain stream never wavered. "I've got all the qualifications—money, stability, solid background, good reputation.'' He grinned, though it seemed a little forced. "Even got all my teeth.''

Her shocked laughter died out quickly. "I don't get it. What's in it for you?''

He clucked his tongue. "Such a cynic.'' But she caught the hollowness in his eyes as he glanced away.

"Michael, this is ridiculous.''

His gaze clicked back to hers. "But it solves your problem, doesn't it?''

"Yeah, and unleashes about a zillion more. We can't even be in the same room without arguing. We're as different as night and day. You've got a different future. One of these days you're going to fall in love with one of the babes you've always got stashed away, have a rich baby or two and live the perfect life in a perfect house.''

"No.'' His jaw flexed. "I'm not falling in love again. Not ever. That's over for me.'' For one instant, something dark and wounded peered out from deep inside his eyes. Quickly he shuttered them, so quickly she might have imagined it.

The very thought shocked her. She'd never thought of Michael Longstreet as anything but on top of his game. That was the man everyone knew: easy to laugh, comfortable inside his skin, a confident leader of men. She'd never thought his razor-sharp mind capable of being clouded by the messy emotions real people felt.

"What do you mean 'again'?"

One sharp glance told her the topic was closed for discussion. He shrugged, then flashed her the old killer grin she'd seen charm any number of women since she'd first met him. She'd never thought of it as hiding anything but idle rich-boy carelessness before.

"Don't change the subject. It would solve your problem, right?" he asked.

Suzanne blinked, then shook her head. "Why would you do such a thing? Especially for me. You don't even like me."

"That's not true." His tone was emphatic. "I never said that."

"You didn't have to."

He shoved his plate away and leaned closer. "I like your mind." When she snorted, he didn't give. "No, it's true. I respect your mind and your passion for what you do. I don't have to agree with your approach in order to respect you or to know that you're motivated by the best of intentions."

"Then why are you so often the roadblock for my ideas?"

"Because you're impulsive and you let your heart rule your head. You go off half-cocked. You can't expect the whole world to fall in line simply because it feels so right to you. People don't work that way."

"You are so wrong." Suzanne's temper spiked.

Then she heard him chuckle.

One dark eyebrow lifted as she illustrated his point perfectly.

She shoved her fingers into her hair. "It would never work. We'd kill each other and Bobby would be an orphan again."

His eyes softened. "I don't think it would go quite that far, as long as we gave each other wide berth."

A spark of hope glimmered. "So it would all be a sham? We'd only pretend to be married?"

"We'd have to make it legal. I'd imagine Jim's cousin would check. You'd have to live with me."

"Not forever, though. Just until I could adopt Bobby legally. Then she could never take him."

"We'd have to both adopt him. The courts aren't going to give custody in a situation where the husband doesn't want to be involved. As a birth mother who has terminated her rights in order for him to be adopted in the first place, you're no different in the eyes of the court than Joe Blow off the street."

She knew it was true, but hearing it from him was like a knife blade to the pain she'd carried around ever since the day she'd signed those papers.

"I don't understand you at all. Why would you want to do this?"

His jaw tightened. "I have my reasons."

"Uh-uh. No dice, Rich Boy. I had to spill my guts, now you start talking, too."

For a moment his eyes looked hard and cold as ice. He glanced away, then sighed deeply. He studied the scarred tabletop as he spoke. "My father has been ill for many years. Ever since I was twelve and he had a massive heart attack, his health has been precarious and every day was a bonus. For too many years I forgot that, but I've tried to make it up to him since I moved back." He glanced up quickly through thick brown lashes. "He had pneumonia this winter, and it put a terrible strain on his already-damaged heart. His doctor says he's weakening pretty dramatically lately. I can see it myself."

He stopped and toyed with his glass of iced tea, skimming wet circles on the table. She tried not to notice his long fingers, his capable hands. Then he looked at her squarely. "He wants badly to see me settled, wants to see me happily married and building a future like the one he's always wanted for me."

"But I can't—"

He shook his head vigorously. "Don't worry. That's not going to happen. That's not my future. I like my life just fine as it is."

"So what is this, Michael? Why are you talking to me about—"

"I could give him the illusion. That's little enough for me to do. I can't do anything else for him anymore, but I could do this. I could give him a reason to think that the future he's convinced I need is within reach. He won't last long enough for me to give him a grandchild, but I could give him the hope, if you'd help me."

"What about Bobby? I couldn't stay married too long. I wouldn't want Bobby to get attached to you."

"Don't worry. I'll be careful. He's young enough not to care about the legal issues. I'll just be a friend. I actually like kids a lot." There it was again, that swift stab of pain in his eyes. "But I won't try to win your son over. And as soon as permanent custody is granted and my dad is gone, we can get a painless divorce. I'll pay child support—I can afford it. I wouldn't want your son to suffer because of any of this."

She stiffened. "You aren't going to buy me off. I'm through with rich boys buying their way out of things."

"I'm not the rich boy who hurt you, Suzanne. If monthly support isn't acceptable, then let me give you a settlement for his college education."

"This isn't about money. If we did this crazy thing, I'd be responsible for all my expenses and Bobby's."

A tiny smile flickered on that too-handsome face. "I doubt you make enough to pay my electric bill."

"I'm not going to be indebted to you for money." Just as she felt temper flaring, she beat it back. He was being decent, and her pride was striking out.

Suzanne reached across the table for his hand. The feel of his skin jolted her, made her very aware of the reality of what she was doing. But she was also deeply grateful. "I'm sorry. I'm just not used to leaning on other people. I can't lean on you. If I could do this alone, I would, but you're right. It's a god-send. I don't want your money, though. It's enough—more than enough—that you'd do this to help me get back my son.''

She could feel tears threatening, but she couldn't give in. In the morning they'd probably both decide that the whole idea was insane. But just in case, she had to set the ground rules.

"Separate bedrooms. If my money won't go far enough, we'll keep an account. I'll pay you back somehow. I'll play whatever part is needed to convince your father." She drew a deep breath. "And no settlement at the end.''

A muscle in his jaw jumped. "You can't tell me what to do with my money. If I want to set up a college fund for the boy, I'll damn well do it.''

"You will not—'' She exhaled in a gust and fell back against the booth. "This is hopeless. It would be worse for Bobby to go into a home where there's fighting than to be with Jim's cousin.''

"I never took you for a quitter,'' he said, settling back against the booth. But his eyes bored into her. "It's not hopeless unless you let it be. Difficult, yes, but not hopeless. We'll put on a great show in public and give each other wide berth in private.''

"And what will Bobby think? He'll be there in private with us.''

"We'll keep things very civil and pleasant. You can restrain yourself enough to do that, right, Suzanne?'' His gaze dared her to admit she lacked self-control. "I'll be good to the boy, I told you that. You'll give him the love he needs. You're the expert on children, and you want to raise him alone anyway. If he doesn't get attached to me, it will make things easier in the long run. But that doesn't mean he and I can't be friends.'' His smile was wry. "Believe it or not, any number of people seem to think I'm pretty good at being a friend.''

Shame washed over her. He was making her a very generous offer, giving her a path to a dream she'd held so long that it had woven itself into the fiber of her soul. She could have her son back, and all she had to do was to pretend to be happily married to Michael when they were out in public.

He wasn't an ogre. He never had been. They didn't see eye to eye on politics, but he'd never been unkind to her. There was more than a little truth in his assessment—she led with her heart, always had. Just because he didn't wasn't wrong, it just wasn't her way.

"What if you're wrong?'' she asked. "What if you're crazy about Bobby and don't want to let me have him?''

"That—'' his voice grew tight "—will not happen.'' He huffed out a breath. "Look, Suzanne, if you want me to put it in writing, I will. I don't want a family. I don't need one.''

"Why not?'' She'd often thought him some sort of

Casanova, some perpetual playboy with an Ivy League mind. Now she knew she'd judged him too quickly. There was a story here, and she wanted to know it.

"I had a family I loved very much. They're gone. End of story."

She'd heard once that he'd been a widower for years, but no details. "What happened?"

She was shocked to see his eyes hollowed out by grief. "I don't want to discuss it."

Shame washed over her again. "I'm sorry, Michael." She reached for his hand, but he jerked it away.

There was pain here, and it was deep. Why had she never suspected? He'd perfected his cover, that was why. She had bought the fiction of a man who was everyone's friend, whose life was a breeze.

"Don't look at me like that," he said. "I'm fine. It's over."

He was dead wrong. He'd erected barriers fathoms deep and oceans wide, but he hadn't dealt with his grief, merely buried it.

His demeanor made it abundantly clear that the topic wasn't up for discussion. And truthfully, he'd just given her the best assurance she could have that he wouldn't want to claim her son. He had a child of his own who still resided in his heart, alive or not.

She should accept this boon for what it was—a very generous gift. He had reasons to need this marriage and so did she. They were reasonable people. And it was only for a little while. Only temporary. She'd lived with a hole in her heart for ten years. She'd have her child back, the child she'd never quit missing. She could play her part in the charade that would make that possible.

"All right. I think we understand each other and what we need and don't need, what we want and don't want. You'll help me get my son, and I'll help you make your father happy. As soon as possible, we'll go our own ways, but in the meantime, we'll deal together as reasonable people and try to make it as easy on each other as we can. Deal?" She held out her hand.

His mood lightened. His mouth quirked in a grin. "You won't strain something trying to be reasonable, will you?" He closed his large, warm hand over hers, and she felt the jolt again.

"It depends. Do you leave wet towels on the bathroom floor?"

He laughed then, dimples winking, his even white teeth flashing. For one second, something inside her shivered as his very maleness swamped her.

"No. I have my faults, but that's not one of them."

She pulled her hand away, but she could still feel the heat of him buzzing beneath her skin. "Have we lost our minds, trying this?"

"Probably. But let's do it anyway." He stood and extended his hand to her. "Walk out with me. We need to get started convincing people that we're a couple.''

Hesitantly, she slipped her hand in his, let him tug her to her feet.

But he didn't stop there. He pulled her into his arms and before she could react, lowered his mouth to hers.

The kiss was quick but lethal. Michael lifted his head and stared at her, his own confusion mirroring hers.

Suzanne knew she should pull away, but she couldn't seem to do it. The sense of safety in his strong arms was seductive. It felt far better than it should.

Mistake, her mind kept trying to say to her.

But before her voice could catch up, Michael lowered his mouth to hers once more.

And this time it wasn't quick. It wasn't casual.

It was more lethal. Devastating. When one arm tightened around her and the other hand slid into her hair, Suzanne felt her legs turn to jelly, her brain overload.

All the fire that had sparked between them in words in the past raced to a four-alarm blaze when they touched. As though they belonged to someone else, her arms slid around his trim waist, her hands sliding over the long muscles of his back, her mouth surrendering to his, her body softening against him.

Her response was gasoline splashed on flames. His

powerful body tightened against her, and she thought she heard someone moan softly before she realized it was her own voice.

Michael broke off the kiss and let her go, then quickly pulled her back. She'd seen those green eyes in many guises, but she'd never seen them hot. And bewildered. Very much like her own must be.

Suzanne shivered. Michael dropped his arms and stepped back.

"This—" His voice was rough. It felt like sandpaper on her too-sensitized skin. "This could be a problem."

She realized that many patrons had turned their way. Bobby, she thought. My baby. Nothing else mattered.

"It won't happen again," she said, furious that her voice was shaking.

Michael studied her for a long moment, his expression moving from stunned to almost amused. The heat still simmered in his eyes. "Spontaneous combustion is a force no one can control."

There were many more facets to Michael Longstreet than she'd seen. She'd need every bit of her wits to pull off this charade.

She struggled to remember the Suzanne Jorgenson who'd traded barbs with him with abandon in council chambers. "Heat lightning," she said. "It comes, but it doesn't last. And it doesn't come often." She shrugged with an assurance she wished she felt.

One dimple winked at her. The smile was too much. No way would she check to see if the eyes were still smoldering.

"Don't kid yourself, Suzanne. We'll strike fire off each other. Often." But to her relief, he shrugged and clapped a companionable arm around her shoulders. "But it's just sex. And we're reasonable people, right?"

She thought she heard laughter in his voice, but she wasn't looking at him again tonight. That was too dangerous by half.

So she just patted the hand that lay on her shoulder and smiled for the audience. "Reasonable, that's right. Now get me the devil out of here."

Michael laughed and led her outside.

# Three

———

Warm rays of sunlight on his face awakened Michael. He levered himself up from the bed, not happy that he'd overslept. A glance at the clock told him he'd have to hurry to squeeze in his morning run. He scrubbed his face with both hands, then slid them upward through his hair.

And then it hit him.

He fell back on the mattress, arms outspread. The night—and his impulsive gesture—came flooding back.

He was going to get married. To Suzanne Jorgenson.

Jerking upright, he pulled on a pair of ancient

sweats and shoved his feet into his running shoes. He barely spared a glance for the treasured panorama from his bedroom but as he crossed to the hallway door, his gaze fell on the connecting door that led from his bedroom to an old-fashioned dressing room…and then to the bedroom Suzanne would have. The house had been built by a San Francisco shipping magnate in the last century and it had four bedrooms, two large and two small, all on the second floor. He used one of the smaller ones for an office, and the boy would need the other, which left only the room originally designed for the magnate's wife.

Separate bedrooms had seemed perfectly reasonable last night, but that was before that last kiss. Now he wondered if maybe these weren't separate enough.

Michael began his warm-up stretches, his mind lost in thought.

He should have expected it, he guessed, that swift punch of need. It was an understandable reaction to the wealth of passion he'd already seen in Suzanne's devotion to her causes. He had to admit that he'd wondered, sitting there on the dais watching her eyes spark as she argued fervently over one thing or another, if that fervor would translate to the physical.

He'd underestimated how much. And seriously underestimated his own reaction to it. The woman would strip a man of every rational thought and leave him happily witless.

Suzanne might be small, but she packed a punch.

But that wasn't the part that worried him most. For all that she could make a man want, it was the new vulnerability he'd seen in her that gave Michael pause. This was a dangerous game they would play—assuming she wasn't having second thoughts as huge as his.

He'd have to track her down this morning and take a good look in her eyes. Given how badly she wanted her son, he suspected she'd go ahead, no matter her doubts. And he'd given his word, so he wouldn't retract his offer.

He finished his last stretch and cast one more look at that connecting door.

Shaking his head, he pounded down the stairs. He'd hate to drill into the antique doors, but locks were made to control temptation, if he needed them. Kissing Suzanne last night had been an impulse but a very good lesson. Having her close would be a constant physical temptation, but he had his warning.

He'd have to be very careful. A woman like that could make a man lose his head. Good thing he wasn't a man who let his body rule his mind.

But that kiss, that feel of her pressed against him—

No. Suzanne needed his help, and he was a man of his word. If she still wanted to go through with it, he would not let her down nor let physical attraction complicate an already thorny situation.

He raced out the front door and let the cold air slap sense into him.

\* \* \*

Suzanne slipped out of the last room housing one
of her charges and walked down the hallway of Emily's House, already thinking about Monday's move
of the kids to Hacienda de Alegria, the Colton ranch.
Mentally compiling her to-do list, she was lost in
thought when she heard his voice. Her gaze arrowed
toward the man who'd made last night a very bad one
for sleep.

Michael stood with a couple of staff members and
Dr. Jason Colton, patiently answering questions about
the water crisis. He hadn't seen her yet, so Suzanne
was free to look her fill. She needed to do it, to put
him into some perspective. To remember that he was
merely extending a helping hand in return for her help
in solving his own problem. That was all this was,
nothing else. A simple, bloodless, temporary marriage
that each of them needed for different reasons.

If only he didn't look so good. Dressed in his usual
jeans and boots and wearing a long-sleeved forest-
green shirt, he held his leather jacket over his shoulder with two fingers. Tall and so at ease in his skin,
he smiled and laughed easily as he talked with the
trio.

She wondered if anyone else in Prosperino knew
he was a fraud. That Mr. Romeo Rich Guy had a heart
that had never healed after a loss he refused to discuss.

She wanted to know what had happened, but he'd
made it very clear that the topic was off limits. And

maybe it was better that way, she thought as she watched his dimples flash around a smiling mouth.

Because that mouth was a problem. Suzanne lifted one hand and pressed her lips, still able to feel the touch of his.

No wonder he had hot and cold running women. The man could kiss...oh, how he could kiss. She'd have to add one more item to the list. Separate bedrooms weren't enough.

No kissing. No touching. Only her son could matter, and her plans were clear. She needed this sham of a marriage only until she could make Bobby hers again. Michael had promised to keep his distance, but she could already feel how keeping her own could become a problem.

Just then he looked up and saw her. Quickly she dropped her hand, but she couldn't seem to move.

He said something to the group and shook hands with Dr. Colton, but he hardly took his eyes off her. With that long ambling stride of his, he headed in her direction, his gaze holding her in place.

"Good morning," he said, the smooth baritone voice sliding easily over her jangled nerves.

She slid one finger beneath her hair and tucked it behind her right ear, gripping the strap of her purse tightly with her other hand. "Good morning."

He studied her. "You didn't sleep. You need to rest, Suzanne. You're worn out."

Why was it he could make her temper kick up so

easily? "I'm perfectly fine. You needn't worry about me." She subjected him to the same perusal. "How did you sleep?"

The broad shoulders shrugged. "I slept great. Overslept, in fact."

Damn him. He did look rested, at least more so than she felt.

A long pause ensued.

Michael broke it. "Have you had breakfast?"

She shook her head. "I'm not much on eating first thing in the morning."

"Well, I'm starved. I only had an apple after my run." He held out a hand. "Come have breakfast with me and we'll make plans."

Carefully, she avoided touching him. Taking his hand last night was where the problem started. "I'm not really hungry, but I suppose we do need to talk."

Michael's smile was too perceptive. He walked beside her down the hall and leaned closer. "So you're not chickening out?"

Suzanne turned to look at him. "Are you?"

He hesitated for a moment, then shook his head. "No. Not if it's still what you want."

What *she* wanted? Did she want this? She wanted her son, yes, but if there were any other way...

"Calculating your options?"

She saw his knowing smile. Why did he have to be so big, so thoroughly male? Feeling the heat of his big body beside her, she was thrown back into last night, into how safe she'd felt tucked against him.

Safety was seductive, a luxury she couldn't afford. The last time she'd felt safe, she'd been fifteen and wildly in love. It had been her last fling with innocence, with wholehearted abandon. The price had been high. Too high.

She settled for honesty. "I wish I could see an option, but I can't. Only giving up Bobby, and I won't do that again. What about you? Surely you've come to your senses and know how insane this is."

"I gave you my word, Suzanne. I don't welsh on commitments." Her hair had swung out from behind her ear as she turned. With one long finger, he tucked it back.

Her breathing deepened. Everything stood still.

Then someone opened the door beside them. With a jolt, she blinked as if awakening from a dream.

Michael broke the contact, putting out one hand to hold the door open for her.

Suzanne brushed past him, very, very careful not to touch.

They were back in Ruby's. Back in the same booth. But not the same people they were last night.

Michael sipped his coffee and studied the woman across from him. She was no longer in despair, but she was nervous. Really nervous. Her napkin was twisted and shredded on the ends.

"Suzanne, you don't have to be afraid of me. I promise I'm not an ogre."

Her head jerked upward. "I'm not afraid of you."

"Look, we don't have to do this, you know. It's going to be tough enough if we cooperate. Being at odds will only make things harder."

She dropped her napkin and exhaled. "I know. I'm sorry. I just—" She stopped, stared behind him. Her face underwent a major change into horror, and she leaned forward, whispering. "Oh, no. Here comes Homer Wentworth's wife."

Michael leaned toward her. "Then I'd say we'd better put on a good show for the town gossip if we want to sell that we were overcome by passion and couldn't wait." He picked up her hand and kissed her fingertips. When she sucked in a quick breath, he reminded himself that this was all for show.

"Is she still looking?"

"Hmm?" Suzanne stiffened and looked behind him. "Oh. Yes."

"Then you might want to smile as though you like it."

"Right." Quickly she treated him to a blinding smile.

He squeezed her hand and tried to ignore the jolt that accompanied every time he touched her. "That's good. Maybe a little contrived, but—"

Suddenly she leaned across the table and put her mouth on his.

Just as quickly, she sat back on her seat, her violet eyes wide and a little too bright.

He knew how she felt. Maybe if they kissed a lot, it would get ordinary.

Yeah, right.

She arched one raven eyebrow. "Was that more convincing?"

Michael had to chuckle. Damned if he'd let her know that the punch landed straight to the gut. Whimpering might have been tempting, but it wouldn't do for the mayor to howl at the moon. Especially on a bright Wednesday morning. "Yeah." He exhaled forcefully. "That should work."

"So," she said with the faintest quiver in her voice. "How shall we do this?"

"I think Tahoe is our best bet. This weekend. We spend the rest of the week showing people that the sparks they've seen flying at council meetings have turned to something new, so it seems in character. Scales falling from the eyes, that sort of thing. We got under each other's skin and one day we realized why."

Her eyes were huge and uncertain as she studied him, but after a moment she nodded and looked down at her coffee cup. "I suppose that's the best angle, some sort of physical reaction that got out of control. We can pretend that it's true, that we got swept away. Then when it's over, we'll just say that we were too hasty. Didn't take enough time to know the other as a person.''

Pretend that it's true? There was too much truth in it for comfort. She was lying to herself if she said otherwise. The body doesn't lie, and he'd felt her respond to him. She couldn't have missed his response to her.

But let her lie to herself all she wanted. It would make it easier for him to keep his hands to himself except in public.

''Yeah.'' He nodded sagely and resisted a smile. ''So how about if I make arrangements in Tahoe for Saturday? We can leave that morning and be back that afternoon.''

''It's close to a five hour drive. We'd need to leave early.''

''We'll be there in less than an hour. We'll take my plane.''

She blinked, then her eyes widened. ''You have your own plane?''

He shrugged. ''It has its uses.''

Her voice cooled noticeably. ''Right. Useful.''

''What?'' He didn't like her look.

''Nothing.'' She glanced away.

''What, Suzanne? Remember Mrs. Wentworth behind us. It doesn't look good for you to be scowling at me. That's the old routine, remember?''

She glanced past him and pasted on a smile.

"That's better. Now tell me what the problem is. Are you afraid to fly?"

She shook her head.

"Afraid to fly with me? I'm a good pilot. Not one accident, and I've been flying since I was sixteen. I'll take good care of you, I promise."

"It's not that."

"Then what is it? What's the problem?"

She dropped the smile and leaned closer. "You're really rich, aren't you? Not just well-off but honestly rich."

He shrugged. "I'm not Bill Gates, if that helps."

"It doesn't."

"So what do you want me to do about it?"

"Nothing. It's just that people will think I'm marrying you because you're rich."

He leaned closer. "Suzanne, I have a news flash for you. You *are* marrying me because I'm rich." With a chuckle, he slid one hand into her hair and kissed her quickly, then let her go and tried to dodge the punch to his senses. "I guess it's up to you to convince people it's my body you're truly after."

He grinned, but it wasn't funny, the corner they'd painted themselves into.

But laughing seemed the only solution.

On Saturday, Suzanne heard the knock on the door of the tiny garage apartment where she lived. She glanced in the mirror one last time and saw her blood-less cheeks.

Was she crazy? She was about to marry a man she barely knew, a man with whom she had nothing in common but a need to appear to be happily married. It certainly wasn't her girlish dream of her wedding day. She'd imagined the long white dress, the orange blossoms, the tall, handsome groom who was crazy in love with her.

Michael Longstreet was tall and handsome, but that was the only similarity she could find.

He knocked again, and she snapped shut her lipstick and left the tiny bathroom, not even stopping to check her appearance in the mirror. If she let herself reflect on the difference in this deep purple wool dress and the long white gown of her dreams, she was afraid she would break down.

Today was for Bobby's sake. That was all that could matter. Even as she thought of his name, his dear face leaped into her mind, the black hair like her own, the blue eyes of his father. The precious sprinkle of freckles over his nose. He would be taller than her, thank goodness. Already his head came up to her shoulder.

She would walk over hot coals for her child. She would never, ever leave him again. She should count herself lucky that Michael Longstreet's need for her help in his own masquerade dovetailed so nicely with hers.

That settled, she drew in a deep breath, crossed to the door and opened it.

With just one tiny hitch, her heart settled back into its normal beat. Yes, Michael looked wonderful in the camel sweater that brought out the rich brown of his hair, the bright streaks sunlight had left. Yes, his mossy green eyes and thick lashes tugged at her, pulled her toward the drowning pool of his appeal.

But today wasn't about Michael's sex appeal, potent as it was. It was about Bobby. Only Bobby. So Suzanne worked up a neutral smile. "I'm all ready." She turned away to retrieve her purse and coat.

Michael snagged her arm and turned her back toward him. "You look really nice." He glanced down at his jeans. "I've got a suit in the car, but it's easier to pilot a plane in comfortable clothes."

She shrugged. "It doesn't matter."

"It does to me." From behind his back, he retrieved a small, perfect nosegay of violets, delicate lace flaring out from the edge. "You've never been married before, right?"

Too shocked to speak, she took them from his hand and brought them to her face. She shook her head while she breathed in the delicate fragrance.

"You'll have the wedding you want one day, but there's no reason this day has to be stark and sterile."

Suzanne glanced up and found golden flecks around the pupils of his mesmerizing green eyes. Her heart flooded with an unfamiliar emotion. She swallowed hard. "This is very kind." She batted back the tide that would swamp her if she let it. It would be foolish to see this as more than the gesture of a man who had dealt well with many women. "This isn't a real wedding day, but I appreciate your thoughtfulness."

He studied her for a long moment. She stood there under his perusal and fought the urge to shrink away. There was something very serious in those eyes, something that tugged deeper than she wanted to feel.

"You can still back out, Suzanne. No harm, no foul."

Her gaze narrowed. "Do you want me to back out?"

His answer didn't come quickly. Then he shook his head and exhaled loudly. "I don't know what I want." His grin was wry as he rubbed one hand over the back of his neck. "I want to make my father happy. I want to help you with your son. But this feels so—"

"Calculated?" she supplied.

He dropped his hand and his eyes showed his appreciation. "Yeah. I never thought of myself as a romantic. Hell, I'm a lawyer. Logic is my life." He grinned then, that slashing white smile that brought out those devastating dimples. "But I'm not big on taking vows I don't intend to fulfill."

She understood completely. His admission warmed the chill that had settled in her bones. "I know. I feel the same way.'' She took another whiff of the violets to steady herself.

"How about if we look at it this way?'' she said. "We'll do our best to live up to the vows we can until it's time for this pact to end. We don't love each other, and we can't pretend that we do. But we can honor and respect each other and do our best to deal well together, knowing that we're really doing this for other people who need us.''

He gazed at her intently, but he didn't speak.

She wasn't sure why she needed to convince him; perhaps the argument was one she needed to hear. "We are doing a good thing, Michael. We're trying to help people we love, and love demands sacrifices. I think I can live with the difference between this day and a real marriage if you can, knowing that it's the only way I can do the right thing by my son. Is knowing how happy your dad will be enough reason for you?''

Michael smiled, and this time his eyes held a fondness she hadn't seen before. "Yeah.'' He exhaled and his shoulders settled. "I think it is.'' He didn't touch her, but his gaze was almost a caress. "Thanks, Suzanne. That helps. I wasn't comfortable wondering if I was rushing you into something you'd regret.''

She smiled then. "We may both regret this heartily before we're done, but it doesn't change the fact that it's what we need to do, that we're doing it for good reasons.''

The dimples flashed again. "The strain of not arguing may kill us."

"I have no intention of not arguing with you. You're wrong too often."

Michael laughed. "That's the Suzanne I know." He walked past her and picked up her coat. "All right, Ms. Jorgenson. Your chariot awaits."

The time for second thoughts was past. Suzanne picked up her purse, took one more sniff of the violets for courage and took her first steps into a future that was anybody's guess.

# Four

She sat in the passenger seat, stiff as a board, her fingers clutched tightly around the violets. She was so damn delicate, despite her fierce will.

"I really am a good pilot, I swear," Michael said soothingly.

Her dress was simple and almost severe, her hair done up tightly in a sophisticated twist. But tiny tendrils escaped around her neck and ears, reminding him that beneath this too-still woman lived the firebrand he thought he knew. She turned his way.

"I'm sure you are. I've just never flown so…close to the ground." She glanced away. "Really, it's very interesting." But her voice quavered, just a bit.

"You're afraid of heights."

She started to shake her head, then glanced at him, a tiny glint in her eyes. "Unfortunately, yes. Somehow this seems so...real. I've flown before, but never on such a small plane."

Michael wanted to laugh. His Bonanza was not considered small, especially compared to his first plane, a Piper Cub. But it was no 757, that was for sure. You felt the experience in this, instead of the distant feeling a jumbo jet conveyed. "You could close your eyes and go to sleep."

"Oh, no. I don't think that's likely." Her lips turned up slightly. "Actually, I want to like it. I'm just not good at looking down."

"So you'd just as soon I didn't do logrolls, I guess."

He saw her swallow hard, but her grin was brave. "Unless you just really need to do one, I think I'll pass."

Michael laughed. He'd never expected to like her this much. "I think I'll survive."

She drew in a deep breath, and he tried not to notice how the soft purple wool clung to her very lovely curves. "Thank you."

Before too long, they were on approach to the small Tahoe airstrip. He explained the mechanics of what they were doing, and she took it all in, asking intelligent and probing questions. It wasn't really a surprise; Suzanne was a very intelligent woman. Only a very smart mind could tangle so successfully with his own as often as she had done in the past.

They touched down, and he heard Suzanne's heart-felt sigh of relief.

He laughed. "I told you I'd get you here safely."

She grinned. "And I believed you. It's just that—"

"I could teach you to fly, you know." What was he offering? They wouldn't be together that long.

"I don't—" Her eyes sparked. "Really?"

That was also the Suzanne he thought he knew. Bold and adventurous. "You'd have to study. How are you at math?"

Her chin tilted. "I'm good. Well, pretty good." She glanced over. "Okay, not great."

He laughed. "You'll have to look down some-times. You ready for that?"

"I might surprise you."

Oh, you do that already, Suzanne. "Once we get back and you get settled in, we'll see if you can spare the time."

She went suddenly quiet. He concentrated on taxi-ing to the terminal. Finally, she spoke. "Michael?"

"Yeah?"

"I've never seen your house. Will I—" She paused. "Will I fit there?"

He thought back to her apartment, which, though small, burst with life, from the plants she had at every window to the quilt folded over her sofa. His house had been constructed with fine craftsmanship, but he'd never made it as much a home as she had done with a tiny place she couldn't even call her own. "You know that quilt on your sofa?"

Her gaze shifted to his. "Yes."

"I think my house has needed something just like that. And I've got lots of windows for your plants, if you want to bring them." He realized they still had many details to handle. "Are you worried about giving up your apartment?"

Her shoulders shrugged. "A little. Prosperino doesn't exactly have a surplus of housing."

Damn. His impulse kept sending ripples through both their lives. "When it's time—" He brought the plane to a stop and turned to her. "When it's time for us to part, I won't ask you to leave until you've found the right place for you and Bobby. All right? Even if it takes awhile."

She nodded. "All right. I appreciate that, Michael. But I won't be picky."

He realized that she'd probably summed herself up pretty neatly in that one sentence. She expected everything of herself, but little of anyone else. It was a wise philosophy, one on which they could agree completely.

"Well." He cut the engine and stirred in his seat. "You ready?"

He didn't expect the quick grin, but maybe he should have. Suzanne Jorgenson was many things he didn't understand, but one of them was not faint of heart.

"Ready as I'll ever be." She reached for her purse and coat.

"Wait, let me help you out." The Bonanza's design had a door only on the passenger side, so he had to crawl over her. He did it with care, but there was no escaping the scent of her perfume rising from the heat of her body, the brush of her hair on his cheek. It would be so easy to pause, to close the faint distance between them....

Damn. He moved past her with haste and jumped down, then turned to lift her out. Hands easily spanning her waist, he lowered her carefully to the icy ground.

Neither one moved. The heat of her warmed his hands, and he found himself tempted to bend toward that beautiful, expressive mouth. Sooty eyelashes swept down to veil her pansy-dark eyes. Her hands tightened on his biceps, but he heard the small whimper of distress escape from her.

It was the dash of cold water he needed.

Mistake. Mistake, Longstreet. Let her go. Now.

Michael released her and stepped back, then focused on securing the plane.

The one time she'd forced herself to look down, Lake Tahoe had been a perfect sapphire blue, and she'd seen the dusting of snow on the treetops, the soft white of the ski slopes. Suzanne stared out the window of the manager's office at the small air terminal, watching unexpected snowflakes begin to fall and wishing she'd brought her boots. The plain black pumps she wore would never hold up if the snow picked up, but Michael had checked before they left, and snow wasn't expected until sometime tomorrow.

But thinking about snow wasn't working as a distraction. In a few more minutes they'd be standing in some anonymous chapel, saying vows they would later break. Yes, couples did that all the time, but at least they started out thinking ''till death do us part'' meant exactly that.

She couldn't worry about that, she thought, brushing her fingers over the nosegay of violets, nor regret that she would not be wearing some stunning white confection. Michael had brought a suit and was changing now, but she would wear this simple wool dress. There was no one to impress, no sentimentality to appease.

This was a simple, straightforward arrangement. A marriage of convenience that they would both forget one day down the road when each of them found their true mate of the heart.

That would be the time for beautiful gowns and bowers of blossoms, not this. But she couldn't help bringing the violets up to her nose and enjoying the delicate scent. At least her partner in this charade wasn't heartless, no matter what he might say.

"Are you ready?"

She whirled at his voice, then lost the power of speech. She had never missed that he was a decidedly handsome man even in the boots and jeans he wore at his office, at council meetings, virtually everywhere he went.

But she'd never seen this Michael Longstreet. This man could indeed inhabit the halls of power, be invited to the most exclusive clubs, dine with the cream of society. The navy pinstripe suit had to be custom tailored, so sophisticated were its lines, so perfectly proportioned to his body. Blinding white shirt, discreetly elegant tie, a shine on his shoes that could put out the eyes…he took her breath away.

And made her more aware than ever that her dress had come off the sale rack of a no-frills department store.

She flattened one hand on her stomach to stem the jitters. How could she even pretend to belong to this wealthy, sophisticated man?

"Cat got your tongue?" he teased. Sliding the tip of one finger behind his top button, he grimaced. "I almost forgot how much I hate wearing a tie."

The jitters smoothed—a little. "You look like you just stepped off the pages of *GQ*."

He screwed up his face and shuddered. "I've done all of that I intend to do, thank you very much." He walked into the office, and the entire space shrank. He was so big. So larger than life in so many ways.

"You look lovely, Suzanne."

"It's the same dress you've seen me in all morning. Michael, maybe we shouldn't—"

He continued as if she hadn't spoken. "And I've enjoyed looking at you the entire time. The color makes your eyes even more vivid." He stepped closer, let his gaze sweep her face before stopping at her eyes. "I always thought violet eyes were the invention of some marketing person, but yours are honest-to-God violet."

"Michael, this isn't going to work. No one's going to buy that I'm your wife."

One sable brow lifted. "They aren't? Why not?"

"Don't be dense. Look at us."

His gaze swept over her with a thoroughness she felt to her bones. "I see a beautiful woman with skin pale as cream and hair black as midnight. What do you see?"

"I see a Yalie in a Savile-Row suit who owns his own plane. Michael, I'm still paying off my student loans, my car is ten years old and I buy strictly off the sale rack."

"Are you trying to convince me or yourself that we don't suit?" He laughed, but there was little mirth in it. "Suzanne, we already know we don't suit, but it has nothing to do with money. Unless, of course, you intend to make me pay for what the rich kid did to you."

Shame washed over her. She ducked her head.

"No. But you don't understand. Your parents will keel over. They'll hate your choice."

Something dangerous flashed in his eyes. "No, they won't." A muscle jumped in his jaw. "I promise you they'll welcome you with open arms."

"But we'll never convince anyone that—"

"I never took you for a coward, Ms. Jorgenson." He crossed his arms over his chest and grinned broadly. "Am I to understand that the same tigress who's tangled with me vociferously over every possible issue for months is afraid of what people might think?"

"Of course not." She tilted her nose in the air.

"My parents will buy it because it's what they want desperately. Jim's cousin will buy it because we'll put on one hell of a show. And as to the differences between us, frankly, I'm shocked at you. I never took you for a snob."

"A snob? Me? But you're the one who—" Her temper, never docile, was beginning to acquire claws.

"As far as I can tell, my only crime this morning has been complimenting you on a lovely dress, bringing you violets, owning a good suit or maybe all three, but I'll be damned if I can figure out why any of them is a hanging offense. Would you care to explain?" His eyes sparkled with amusement.

"You'd never understand." Primarily because he was right. She was acting like a madwoman. It only made her more upset.

"When you have some spare time, maybe you'll explain for the layman." He chuckled indulgently.

Suzanne saw red. She stabbed his chest with one finger. "Listen, buster, don't you dare patronize me. I'll have you know—"

She didn't get to finish because he grabbed her and pulled her against him. "Maybe John Wayne had it right. There might be only one way to handle a woman with a temper."

He lowered his head and suddenly her mouth was too busy to answer.

For a moment, Suzanne was too stunned to react.

Then she was all too aware of the same quick fire that had raced through her veins before when Michael had kissed her. A part of her wanted nothing more than to yield, to revel in the power of this compelling man's kiss.

But a part of her knew it was the road to disaster.

She put her hands on his chest and shoved. "Stop it, Michael. I don't want this."

Temper flared in his eyes, something she'd never seen before. Heat, hunger…all were there.

But swirling in the mix was the same caution she felt. For a moment his hands tightened on her arms.

Then he stepped away.

"I will concede that it's a bad idea." But just as she started to smile in triumph, he nipped that in the bud. "But you're lying to yourself if you say you don't want it. You want me, Suzanne, and I want you. It doesn't have to be smart. It just is.''

She took one step back and found herself against the window. She hugged her arms around her waist. "It doesn't matter." When she saw the corners of his mouth tilt, she shook her head. "It can't matter. You know that as well as I do.''

"We don't have to make this an endurance contest, Suzanne. Just because we don't intend to stay married doesn't mean we can't enjoy the proximity as long as it's comfortable for both of us.''

She looked for that comfort in his eyes, but she didn't see it. "It's not comfortable, Michael. For either of us.''

The casual grin he displayed to the world came to the rescue. "Ah, but dancing close to the flames is its own kind of pleasure, don't you think?'' His tone was light, his grin disarming. But she could see something there that matched too closely to how she felt. There was danger here.

For both of them.

So she straightened and did them both a favor. "I'm not much for taking foolish risks. And I have a child to consider.''

Shame crept over his face then. She could see the heat give way to reality. All humor left his face, and his eyes turned somber. "You're right. I'm sorry.''

It was so tempting to soften then, but she knew it

would be a big mistake. "So, are we ready to begin this charade?"

Michael looked at his watch. "It's just about time." He turned to leave.

But then he turned back, on his face a curiously hesitant look. "Suzanne, look, I'm sorry. I was out of line. I just—" He stopped then as if unsure how to proceed. "Listen, if we're going to carry this off, there's something I need to give you. Otherwise, my parents will never buy that this is for real."

"What is it?"

He reached into his pocket and retrieved a deep blue velvet bag that looked very, very old and handed it to her. "This is something the brides in our family wear when they're married. It's been a tradition for generations."

She was shocked that her fingers trembled as she tried to untie the braided golden cords. All the time that her fingers worked at the bag, her heart pounded and she tried to find the voice to refuse whatever it was.

Finally, she freed the knot and opened the bag whose nap was worn smooth as silk. She glanced up. "Michael, I don't think—"

He took the bag from her and spread the mouth of it. "Hold out your hands."

She obeyed, and into her palms dropped a cameo of such delicate workmanship that she uttered an involuntary gasp. "Oh, Michael, it's beautiful." Even as one finger traced its contours, she lifted her gaze to his. "I can't possibly— Michael, this would be wrong."

A muscle in his jaw leaped. "I was never allowed to give this to Elaine." His voice went rough. "I don't want to betray its significance either, but if I don't give it to you, my parents will never believe in this match and all of this will be for nothing."

Suzanne felt an almost holy stillness, a kind of reverence for this piece and its tradition that shook her to her bones. She looked up at him again. "I don't know what to do."

"Let me put it on you." His tone darkened. "Please. It comes down from oldest son to oldest son. My father's a good man, and I have to believe that counts for something. Surely my ancestors would understand the reason we're doing this." He stood very still, so still that for this moment, it seemed they were alone in all the world.

Her fingers closed around the cameo, the delicate golden chain dripping through her fingers. Suzanne closed her eyes and whispered a prayer, to whom she wasn't sure. Please, forgive me if this is wrong.

Maybe it was only what she wanted to believe, but in that moment, she felt an answering chord of peace settle deep in her heart. Michael was a good man. He was trying to do the right thing, just as she was.

She opened her eyes and tried to find her voice. "Would you—" She cleared her throat and tried again but could only find a husky whisper. "Would you put it on me, Michael?"

He sighed so softly she might have imagined it. "Turn around," he said, his voice still rough. He took the cameo from her hand and his touch burned her fingers.

She tried not to feel his touch on her sensitive nape, but all along the back of her, she could feel him with every cell in her body. Deep within her, a dread began to grow. She would be changed by this forever, no matter how hard she tried. This was not a man a woman could walk away from and forget.

"Thank you, Suzanne." She felt him press one soft kiss to her nape, and goose bumps shot over her body.

She stepped away to save herself, but she didn't turn back to him until she'd wrestled some measure of control. It was far from easy.

Finally she lifted her head, raised her eyebrows, did her best imitation of a casual tone. "Well now, are we ready?" She could almost pass for ready, as long as she didn't look at him.

"Ready or not, it's time."

She might have heard a hint of strain in his voice, but she couldn't be sure. There was nothing to be gained by looking deeper.

He placed a hand at her waist as he led her to the door.

Suzanne carefully stepped away from his touch.

* * *

Michael escorted Suzanne down the aisle of a lovely little chapel he'd been able to wrangle on such short notice only by the application of a good sum of money and every ounce of charm he possessed. It might be a sham marriage, but it was Suzanne's first and he hadn't wanted it to be sleazy. This place came highly recommended, and he thanked his lucky stars that the minister's wife did the bookings and had a soft spot for romance. He didn't know if Suzanne had realized it yet, but today was Valentine's Day in one of the wedding capitals of the world. Every chapel in Tahoe had been booked for months in advance.

They didn't have long. They were being squeezed in between ceremonies. It made no sense, but he really wanted to do this right. Years from now, he didn't want her looking back and finding the memory sordid, hasty though all of this must be.

She'd looked shocked when the minister's wife had handed her the expensive bouquet he'd ordered, insisting on holding on to the small nosegay of violets, too. As she stood beside him now, he could see that she was pale as water, gripping the flowers for dear life. The Longstreet cameo stood out against the deep purple of her dress. Her eyes were wide, her lush lips pressed together tightly. He touched her elbow and she jumped.

He leaned down. "You look beautiful," he murmured. "Just relax. The firing squad has today off."

Her lips tilted upward. She whispered back. "You look a little pale yourself."

Michael grinned at her jibe. "It's not every day a man marries his fiercest opponent."

A hint of color rushed to her cheeks. "See that you remember that, mister."

They both chuckled softly. Then the minister cleared his throat, and the tension came roaring back.

Even as he listened to the words, Michael shoved away memories of the last time he'd heard them, trying not to compare this day to the one so long ago. He'd been so young. So certain. Ten feet tall and bulletproof.

Silence fell, and he realized it was time for his vows. He risked one glance at Suzanne, and the nerves he saw settled him. He'd always responded well to being needed, and she definitely needed the shield he could provide.

So he carefully locked away memories of a day when these vows had been fresh and new and thrilling. Swallowing hard, he responded. "I, Michael, take you, Suzanne to be my lawfully wedded wife, to have and to hold…"

Suzanne listened to his smooth baritone voice and fought back the urge to weep, to run out of this room this instant. She squeezed Michael's forearm. Bobby, she reminded herself. This is for my son.

Michael placed his right hand over hers, and the

warmth of it helped her settle. She glanced up as he spoke.

He was every woman's dream. Argue though they might, different as night and day, she would never deny that he was a man worthy of respect. The woman who had his love would be fortunate indeed.

But he'd made it clear that no woman would ever have his love. It was dead and buried very far away.

Suddenly he looked down and she realized it was her turn. "I, Suzanne, take you, Michael to be my lawfully wedded husband..."

He held her in his gaze for every single word, and she tried not to wish that the clasp of his hand was for more than holding her in place.

Then the minister asked for the rings and Suzanne started to shake her head and tell him they would have none.

But Michael surprised her. The minister's wife gently pried the flowers from her fingers, and Michael took her left hand in his own. In his fingers he held a stunning band of alternating diamonds and amethysts.

Her startled gaze flew to his, and she started to speak, to refuse it.

His eyes darkened in warning just before he began to speak. "With this ring..."

Suzanne watched the ring slide onto her finger as if crafted specially for her. The lavender of the amethysts offset the icy fire of the diamonds. It was the most beautiful ring she'd ever seen.

Then he held out another ring to her, a simple golden band. She watched him press it into her palm and for one second, she closed her fingers around it.

Then the minister began to speak, and Suzanne held Michael's left hand in her own as she slid the band on his long finger, feeling the heat of his skin as her fingers drifted over his. "With this ring, I thee wed…"

Michael took both her hands in his and kept her facing him as the minister pronounced them married. She could see the intent in his eyes and she knew it would be smarter to turn her cheek toward the kiss that was coming.

But something in those green eyes held her—a fleeting glimpse of pain—and she thought about how hard this must be for him, who had known what it was like to say these words in love.

So Suzanne held her ground and accepted Michael's kiss that sealed their bond. It was a tender kiss with none of the shocking heat that had passed between them before, and she resolved to make this as easy as possible for him.

When he smiled at her, she smiled back. They would one day break this bond and their vows would turn to ash, but she realized that it was not in her nature to disregard them now. For whatever time they must deal together, she would do her best to be the kind of wife a man like Michael deserved.

They thanked the minister and his wife and signed the register, then turned to walk back down the aisle. When they reached the front door, all Suzanne could think was that the hardest part was over, that with some distance between them, they could make this work. "We can head home now. I need to call Jim and tell him that everything's going to be all right. Maybe tomorrow I'll go see Bobby. I can't wait to bring him to Prosperino."

Michael started to nod as he opened the door. He took one glance outside, then closed it and looked back at her. "Well, Mrs. Longstreet, you might have to put those plans on hold."

For a minute, she was too rattled by the name to make sense of the rest of what he said. Then it registered. "What do you mean?"

He held the door open wide so she could see out. The world had turned white while they'd been inside.

"The storm that was supposed to arrive tomorrow appears to have a mind of its own. Sorry to tell you this, but we're not going anywhere tonight."

# Five
———

After the fourth place they tried unsuccessfully to get a room, Michael put his foot down. It was that or do something uncivilized to his wife of only three hours. "You're either staying in the car or letting me carry you the next time we get out of the car, Suzanne. Those shoes are soaking wet, and you're not fooling me that you're not freezing." He'd sell his soul for the change of clothes he'd left on his plane. His own feet were blocks of ice.

"I'm fine," she muttered.

"Your lips are blue. If you'd use that brain of yours, you'd know you're only being stubborn. For two cents I'd buy a rope and tie you to the seat." He put the car into gear and drove carefully toward the only place in town that had a room, according to the most recent desk clerk, who'd taken pity on the newlyweds and called around for him.

"Don't order me around. 'Obey' isn't part of the vows anymore, in case you didn't notice."

"The word would have been wasted on you, anyway," he muttered.

"Why can't we just drive back if the plane can't take off?"

The car fishtailed on a slick spot just then. He didn't bother to answer.

She looked around at the silent streets. "I guess if we'd driven, we'd still have trouble getting out."

"My four-wheel drive would have done all right, I think. Except that we'd just now be getting here and would have been too late for the chapel to fit us in."

Chapel. They were really married. He saw Suzanne's right hand brush lightly over the left where his ring nestled beneath her glove.

The reality of it slammed into her violet eyes. "I can't believe it yet."

He smiled grimly. "Me either." Then he saw the sign and pulled the car under the portico. "Hallelujah, a sheltered entry. I'll let you out here where it's dry while I go park the car."

"Dreamers?" She read the sign. "What is this place?"

"I have no idea. It's the only room left in town,

thanks to the storm. No one else can get out either, but quite a few more had already arrived before the storm.''

She glanced into the lobby, then back at him, her eyes dark and worried. A shiver ran through her. ''We can't stay, Michael. I need to get back. The kids at Hopechest need me.''

''Believe me, I understand.'' He'd cursed Mother Nature more than once himself. He'd made his bold pronouncement of confidence to the townspeople, and he needed to be in Prosperino braving the water crisis along with everyone else, not stuck in Tahoe. ''But we don't have any choice.''

''Separate rooms, right?''

''One suite was all they had.'' He saw the protest forming on her lips. ''They say it's big. There has to be a sofa or something. It's the best I can do.'' He hadn't felt this much at the mercy of fate in a long time.

The reality of what they'd done hit him hard. ''Look, Suzanne, this is just the beginning of negotiating tricky waters. We knew it wasn't going to be easy. But Bobby's worth it, right?''

Her head whipped around, eyes sparking. ''Of course he is. It's only—'' She looked out the windshield, then drew herself up very straight. ''I'm sorry. This is just as hard on you. You have a whole town depending on you.'' She cast him a sideways look from those incredible eyes, placing one hand on his arm. "I'm behaving like a spoiled child. I'm sorry, Michael."

He worked up a smile. The day had been centuries long already, and it was barely three o'clock. "No sweat. Go on inside, and I'll be right there."

She gave his arm one soft pat, then drew her coat around her and got out.

When Michael returned, she was already at the reception desk, her billfold open while the desk clerk tapped away at his keyboard. When he came to stand beside her, he could feel the agitation in her frame. Gently, he folded her billfold closed. "I'll take care of this. *Sweetheart,*" he added for the clerk's benefit.

Furious eyes snapped up to his.

"Is there a problem?" he asked.

The very young clerk shifted on his feet.

"Highway robbery," Suzanne muttered. "Do you know what the rates are in this place?"

"It doesn't matter." He smiled at the clerk and handed him a credit card. "We're grateful you could help us."

The young man shot Suzanne a glance, then Michael.

Michael shrugged. "My wife is careful with every penny." He tried to ignore the muffled burst of rebellion at his side. "It's one of the things I love about her." He placed one hand on Suzanne's arm, holding her still while she trembled beneath his hand.

"Er, yes, sir. If you could initial here by the rate, sir?"

Four hundred fifty a night. Michael had paid more many times, but it had been for a suite in Paris. The Plaza in New York. The Ritz in London.

Quickly, he initialed the rate and shoved the paper back at the clerk, hoping he could stem Suzanne's inevitable outburst until they were no longer in public. He took the key and all but dragged her to the elevator.

Rich boy, he thought he heard her mutter. He ignored it and tightened his grip on her arm.

The elevator doors shut, and she quickly jerked her arm from his hand, placing the width of the elevator between them.

"It won't make a convincing case that we were overcome by passion if you're screaming at me in public," he observed.

"I don't scream." She sniffed.

Michael snorted, then quickly composed his face.

Suddenly, she was right in front of him, poking her finger in his chest. "Look, you may not think anything of that rate, but it could pay my monthly rent. It's obscene. No wonder poor children can't get good health care. No wonder single mothers are on food stamps. No won—"

Violet eyes blazing, raven hair flying in a nimbus, she was magnificent. He yielded to temptation, closing his hands on her arms, pulling her against him.

He took her mouth as he'd wanted to do for hours.

At first she went quiet and still, no doubt in shock. Then she sucked in a breath of outrage, opened her hands on his chest—and pushed. But there was no force behind it.

Michael loosened his arms but didn't let go, sliding his tongue along her lips very, very slowly.

Suzanne's body quivered like a bowstring.

Michael knew he should stop before things got out of hand, but for the life of him, he couldn't conceive of stepping away.

Then, all of a sudden, Suzanne went fluid in his arms, sliding her hands up his chest and grabbing fistfuls of his hair. She opened to him, and Michael lost all sense of where they were. Who he was. Who she was. Nothing was real, nothing but this kiss that had turned into something wild, something dark and hot and sweet.

The door opened, and he heard a gasp from outside.

But it still took effort to end the scorching kiss. He didn't care if the President and all his Cabinet stood outside that door. He had to have her. Now.

Michael opened his eyes for one second and saw a housekeeper grinning madly.

With effort, he gentled the kiss. "Suzanne," he murmured.

"Hmmm?" Her fingers tightened in his hair.

Michael resisted the urge to yelp. "Sweetheart."

He pressed one last kiss to her unfairly sexy mouth, then lifted his head. "We've got company."

"Wha—" Slowly her eyes opened, a pansy-purple so dark he wanted to dive inside and never return.

He nodded to the housekeeper behind her and grinned. "Newlyweds."

The woman smiled broadly. "Don't I know it? You two just go right on ahead. You'll like the Jungle Suite."

Suzanne went ramrod stiff and jerked away, her fair cheeks turning an amazing shade of tomato red. She turned one quick look toward the other woman. "Jungle Suite?"

"All the suites got names, sugar," the woman offered. "You're lucky to get a cancellation on Valentine's weekend. This place is booked solid a year in advance."

He heard Suzanne's little moan and pulled her into his side. "I'm afraid the little woman is a bit overcome by the excitement of the day." He tried not to react when Suzanne stiffened against him. Not even when she dug her nails into his side. "I'll just have to be real gentle with her." He winked at the housekeeper, knowing he would pay for that remark.

The woman's laughter followed them down the hall while Michael tried to keep Suzanne from kicking him in the shins. He had to let her go to open the door, and he barely got her inside before she unloaded on him.

"'The little woman'?" she screeched. "First you want to tie me in the car, then you don't even care that you could feed a family for two months on what you've paid for this—" Turning away from him and getting her first look at the room, she fell abruptly silent.

He didn't have words, either, for what lay before them when he'd flipped on the lights.

He shot Suzanne a glance. Her face went still and that beautiful mouth quivered. He braced himself for tears as she bent over, the fall of her hair blocking his view of her face.

When her shoulders began to quake, he broke the resolve he'd just made to keep his hands to himself and touched her shoulder gently. "Suzanne, it's going to be all right, I swear. We'll get through this."

Suzanne threw her head back and laughter spilled freefall from her lips, a bubbling brook of silvery notes cleansing the tension from the space they shared. "I—don't—believe—this—" She gasped for breath between words, one hand over her mouth as she stared around the room.

Michael's gaze scanned the space, as big as an apartment, and had to laugh, too. Yes, he'd paid this much and more before—but never for anything like this.

The Jungle Suite. Deep green vines tangled with trees, and tropical plants burst with orange and fuchsia blossoms. Everywhere. The walls and ceilings were covered with mirrors, and the headboard of the enormous round bed was covered in a riotous print of purple and fuchsia, tangerine and turquoise.

"Oh, my God." Suzanne's eyes were bright as diamonds as she turned in a circle. "Michael, look at that tub."

He followed her pointing finger. A black marble tub as big as his own whirlpool at home sat in one corner, but this one was heart-shaped. Mirrors surrounded it, along with at least a hundred candles. He went for nonchalance. "The hot water will feel good."

Her eyes widened with shock. "You can't be considering staying here."

"There's nowhere else to stay."

"But I— But we—" She pointed aimlessly. "There are mirrors on the ceiling, for heaven's sake."

"It's a honeymoon suite. What did you expect?" He too wanted to groan. This was a sybarite's dream suite, just this side of cheesy, except that everything was first class in its quality. All too easily he could imagine Suzanne lying on that huge round bed naked, her raven hair spilling over the coverlet like a waterfall of silk.

He wanted to lie on his back on that bed and watch her naked above him while they—

"There's no sofa, Michael." Suzanne's voice intruded rudely on the enticing fantasies that were short-circuiting his brain.

"So?"

"I am not sleeping with you. That's not our deal."

The agitation in her voice cut through the smoke fogging his logic. He cleared his throat and tried to find something in this room that didn't fire his imagination into erotic meltdown.

A panel of switches on the wall. Very utilitarian. Good. He stared at it for a moment before his brain would work to read the instructions.

Laughter erupted from his throat.

"What? What's so funny?"

"A thirty-channel remote control sound system with preset programs from Ravel's Bolero to Madonna's Erotica." He couldn't help the mile-wide grin until he turned and saw her. "Er, not funny." He struggled to frown. "Not funny at all."

"There is nothing humorous about this, Michael."

What kind of music would make this woman melt? he wondered.

"Michael—"

He jerked himself back from a whole new line of fantasy. "Yeah. Right." He cleared his throat again. Reality came crashing in. Suddenly he was as tired as he could remember being in a long time. He hadn't slept much last night. "Look, the bed is huge. You could sleep ten people on that without anyone bothering anyone else."

"I am not sleeping with you. We made rules, remember?"

But I hadn't kissed you when we made those rules. I hadn't felt your body against mine.

She'd felt it, too. He knew that, knew that she remembered the moment when her body had surrendered to his, when she'd lost herself in the same heat lightning that had all but melted his shoes to the floor of the elevator.

He fastened his gaze on hers and dared her to deny what they'd shared.

Her eyes pleaded with him. Silently, they reproved him. There was more at stake than one scorching kiss.

Her little boy. His father. The distance each of them needed to keep, no matter how strong the physical attraction. He'd never heard of Suzanne playing around. She wasn't a woman to just go for great sex, no matter how much Michael was now convinced it would be earth-shaking.

And he couldn't offer her more. He could be her friend, and he could be a skilled and pleasing lover. But he would never, ever share his heart. It wasn't his to give.

Suzanne deserved more. She led with her heart and had from the first day he'd met her. She wasn't a woman with whom you played games and walked away.

"I'll sleep on the floor," he snapped. There was no reason to take out his frustration on her. He gentled his voice. "I won't bother you."

She grew very quiet and sank down on the edge of

the bed, looking defeated. "Maybe we should give this up right now. No one knows yet, so there's no damage to repair." Her slender shoulders sank as though the weight of her dreams was more than she could bear.

"No." Michael's refusal was as instantaneous as it was inexplicable. Then he cursed himself silently and viciously. He'd always had a very healthy sex drive and it had been a long time since he'd had to deny it. Knowing that he would be celibate until this was all over didn't help his mood, but he refused to consider risking shaming Suzanne by seeking another outlet for the hungers she so easily aroused in him. He was a grown man who had shown much discipline in his life. He would deal with this.

So he worked hard on keeping his tone reasonable, despite how his teeth were on edge, his body craving hers. "We can pull this off. You need my help and I need yours. We're two reasonable people. It's simply a matter of taking each step as it comes."

The gratitude that swept over her face made him resolve to keep her at arm's length until they could get out of this place and get back to the safety of their normal lives, where there was no reason to see each other but in passing. But even as that thought comforted him, he felt a small pang of regret for what they could never share.

Maybe one day, when this was all over—

Forget it, Longstreet. She's not a woman to have

affairs. She'll have her life and you'll be free to resume yours. Women included.

Right now he needed to get away from her, clear his head. "Look, why don't you take a bath and a nap? I've got some calls to make. I'll make them downstairs."

She started to shake her head, but he overrode her. "Shouldn't you call Jim and tell him that it's done? You can start making plans about when we can pick up your son."

Her protests died. Her lips curved at the thought. "Sure. I—" She frowned faintly and looked up. "I'll use my calling card."

The temper he'd thought long ago conquered flared as though she'd lit a fuse. "Suzanne, just bill the damn call to the room. Talk for two hours, I don't care." He heard his voice rise but couldn't seem to stop it. "I can afford it, all right? So sue me if you don't like it that I can afford this room and this trip and—" He threw up his hands in disgust. "I'll be back. I'll leave the key with you so you don't have to worry that I'll intrude."

He tossed the key on the bed and left before he could add any more sins to his list.

Suzanne hung up the phone, still smiling broadly after hearing Bobby talk about the new puppy Jim had gotten him. A black Lab named Maverick, the pup had already taken a firm hold on Bobby's heart.

She wondered what Michael would think about inheriting a dog. Jim admitted that it probably wasn't his right to introduce a dog he'd never raise, but he'd wanted Bobby to have something to bridge the gap once he was gone, a piece of his life with Bobby that would still be there for comfort when he could no longer do so himself. Edna Waters, his late wife's cousin, didn't mind dogs as long as they were kept outside, he said.

Jim had had no way to know Michael even existed when he'd gotten the dog.

But they'd cross that bridge when they came to it.

There was a shower in the bathroom, but she eyed the huge whirlpool tub with longing, wondering if she had time to take a quick bath before Michael returned.

A few minutes later, blissfully ensconced in bubbling waters, Suzanne leaned back against the bath pillow and heaved a huge sigh. Over her body, the water swirled, soothing away the nerves of this unique and trying day. Drifting on a tide of relaxation so complete it was almost sinful, she felt her mind begin to wander, too. Eyes closed, she relived the kiss in the elevator, the press of his big muscular body against hers, and longing suffused her. Her body floated with the currents of the whirlpool, and she felt the brush of bubbles over skin that now felt too sensitive, too tight to contain all the heat that Michael could generate with little effort.

She let herself imagine the two of them in this

suite, free of other ties. If it were only them with no other responsibilities, nothing but the long night ahead, so sheltered from the storm...

What did Michael look like beneath his clothes? She'd felt the power of those muscles, knew that he had never used his full strength with her, treating her like some delicacy she'd never been. She was no fragile flower, no pale tea rose. She was a sturdy weed, not all that pretty, not very desirable, but strong. She endured.

He made her feel so feminine, almost dainty. So protected. Even when she knew he was tempted badly, he'd always kept his strength under a tight leash.

But what would it be like if Michael's leash snapped? If he wanted her as badly as he made her want him? In this place, this jungle room, what if she possessed the power to enchant him past bearing? What if they were free to play outside the realities of their world?

Fire raced over her nerves, across her skin, and made her burn. She could almost feel Michael's hands on her body, could imagine sliding over him in this tub, lying beneath him on that huge round bed. Could imagine him poised above her, moss-green eyes gone dark with power—

A knock sounded on the door. "Suzanne?"

She scrambled from the tub so quickly that water shot from the jets and hit the floor. Frantically she fumbled for the switch, then tried to remember where she'd left the robe the hotel provided. She caught a quick glimpse of herself multiplied a hundred times in the mirrors.

"Suzanne, are you all right?"

Naked. Oh, God. "Yes." She gulped, then finally spotted the fluffy white robe. "Just a minute."

Quickly she donned it, her heart racing a mile a minute as she tried to adjust from thinking about—

No. Oh, no. She couldn't let him see. It must be written all over her face. As she walked toward the door, she grabbed a towel, then flipped the lock and turned away, busying herself drying her hair, praying the towel would cover her face until she could compose it.

Michael shoved the door open with his foot, so loaded down with packages that he could barely see where he was going. "Could you take this—" He fell silent.

She was bent over, toweling her hair, and the view of her luscious behind made his mouth go dry. He jerked his gaze away, only to see the front of her reflected in the mirror. Her face was blocked by the towel, but the robe she wore gaped in the front just enough that he could see the upper curve of her breasts, the seductive shadow between.

"What?" she asked, her voice muffled by the towel.

All he could think about was that she was naked

beneath that robe. It took him a minute to recover his powers of speech. "Nothing." Resolutely he walked past her, regret that he couldn't linger and look shadowing every step.

He dropped several of the packages on the bed, holding on to the box of pizza at the bottom and the sack of champagne. Taking them over to the table, he risked one glance in the mirror beside him and couldn't decide whether to cheer or groan that there was hardly an inch of wall space—or ceiling, for that matter—not covered with the reflective means to torture a man who wasn't here for this room's anointed purpose.

He could be. He sure would like to be.

But he wasn't. Couldn't be. If ever there was a woman he needed to keep his hands off of, Suzanne was it.

"There's a hair dryer. Wouldn't it be simpler?" he asked. She was still bent over, toweling her hair. If she didn't stand up straight pretty soon, he was not going to be responsible for his actions.

She didn't answer.

"Suzanne? Hello?"

Finally, she straightened, lowering the towel slowly. Her face was red from being bent over so long, but the flush extended down to where the robe gapped even more.

He turned away. Quickly. Not one of his friends would believe he was trapped for the night with this delectable woman and had no intention of touching her.

Hell, he couldn't believe it himself.

"There's not much to choose from right now. It's too late for lunch and too early for dinner, so I grabbed us a pizza. I hope pepperoni's all right." Not that he cared about the stupid pizza. His mouth was suddenly full of sawdust, and he doubted he could choke down a bite, never mind that he'd been starved until he walked through the door.

"Mushrooms, too?" she asked with a husky undertone in her voice that made him want to howl.

"Yeah. And bell peppers."

"Sounds perfect."

He glanced in the mirror and saw her staring at him with something that looked a lot like hunger. If only he couldn't see the nerves, too. If only he could forget what was real. What she really wanted. What he'd promised.

No, sweetheart, he wanted to say. Perfect would be you and me in that tub. On that bed. Me inside you until we lost our minds.

He was so hard he ached. "Don't look at me like that unless you want to be flat on your back in the next five seconds," he growled.

With a little squeak, she whirled away, her head swiveling from side to side as she looked for refuge. "I'll just put my dress back on. Excuse me, please."

"Don't."

"What?"

Stay naked. My hands could be inside that robe in the next second. I could have you under me in two. He shook his head violently to rid himself of temptation. He started to speak, then had to clear his throat. "I brought you some warm clothes."

"Where did you—" Her lids fluttered down, then rose again. "Did you keep the receipt?"

That cooled his blood as nothing else could. "No," he snapped. "Consider it a wedding present. Dammit, Suzanne, can't you even accept the smallest gesture?"

"Clothes aren't small. A Popsicle is small."

"Well, pardon me, but I thought you'd rather have some warm clothes than a Popsicle. Foolish of me, but there you go. I'm just a stupid rich guy who doesn't get it."

Color glowed brightly in her cheeks, and battle flared in her eyes. The hellion of the council chambers was back.

In a fluffy white robe. He couldn't help smiling.

"What's so funny?" she snapped.

"You. Me. I was just picturing you dressed like that at the next council meeting. A whole new image for Prosperino's own Joan of Arc."

He could see hasty words about to spill from her lips and waited for her to blast him. A fight sounded pretty good right now. He needed some way to dissipate all the heat in his body dying for a far preferable release he didn't have a chance in hell of obtaining.

Then she threw back her head and laughed. A rich, husky laughter that made his blood race. But he'd just have to get used to that. Being with her every day was going to be a delicious kind of hell, he could already see.

But it wouldn't be boring.

Michael laughed along with her. The nerves of the last twenty-four hours, the strain of desire that could not be appeased, the absurdity of this room, this situation...

It was pretty damn funny, he had to admit.

Suzanne collapsed on the bed, tears streaming from her eyes as laughter rolled from her lips, slowly diminishing to giggles. Then she got the hiccups.

Loud ones. Unladylike as hell.

She slapped one hand over her mouth and tried to stifle them, but another one escaped. Michael was laughing until she fell back on the bed, then curled abruptly into the fetal position with a raw moan.

He was across the room in one second, leaning over her. "What's wrong? Are you hurt?"

She shook her head, eyes squeezed tightly shut, arms wrapped around her waist as if in pain.

"Suzanne, tell me what you need."

She was so still. Instinctively, he felt for the pulse in her throat, both of them jumping at the feel of his fingers on her skin.

When he felt the sure, steady beat, he relaxed. But he didn't remove his hand, trailing it instead along the delicate line of her collarbone, knowing he should step away. Now.

Air exploded from her lungs, and he realized she'd been holding her breath. She sucked in one greedy gulp of air, then fell still again.

Her sooty lashes laid on her skin, casting lacy shadows. Silken strands of jet-black hair drifted around her, some of them brushing his fingers as he stroked up her throat, then down again.

Silence painted the room, filled all its corners, a silence fecund and rich with longings unspoken.

Michael couldn't make himself lift his fingers from the sweet satin of her skin. As he trailed them down past the fragile hollow of her throat, he lowered his head, telling himself he'd stop if only she'd say something.

But Suzanne lay unmoving under his hand, a stillness that covered the hum of nerves strained past bearing.

One kiss. Just one kiss would hold him.

Carefully, as though she were a wild animal who had never known a man's touch, he brushed his lips over hers, feeling as much as hearing the soft gasp of her breath, the rising beat of her heart under his hand.

And then she hiccuped again.

She curled up again and hid her face in her arms,

groaning loudly. "I am so embarrassed I am going to climb into these covers and never come out."

The spell broke. With an odd feeling of relief for rescue from what he knew would be a major mistake, he stepped back from the bed and headed for the bathroom to draw a glass of water.

He returned, and she was, if anything, more tightly curled into a ball, her entire body quaking with each hiccup. He grasped one hand and tried to pull her to a sitting position.

She pulled back, shaking her head. "No," she wailed, though he could hear the tinge of humor. "I'm never coming out, I tell you."

Michael felt the most profound relief to be able to joke instead of being eaten alive by a hunger he knew wasn't dead. But it was beaten back for now. "Come on, don't be such a girl."

"I am a girl."

He tugged again. "You're not a sissy girl. Come on, sit up and drink this water."

"It's an old wives' tale. It doesn't work."

"My mother swears by it. Works every time for me."

"I have to hold my breath."

"Doesn't seem to be working." When she hiccuped loudly again, he smiled. "Come on, sit up. Try it. What have you got to lose?"

With a groan, she let him pull her up, grasping her long mane in one hand and smoothing it back from her face. "This—" She hiccuped and grimaced. "This better work. I'm dying."

He handed her the glass, watching her swallow until the movement of her throat drew his attention back to the opening of that damn robe.

Quickly, he turned away and walked to the pizza. He wasn't hungry, but he needed to do something with his hands. He stood there, staring at the box since it wouldn't show him her reflection like every other surface in this godforsaken room. He chewed and swallowed, concentrating so hard that when her arm reached past him for a slice, he nearly jumped out of his skin.

"Jumpy, Mr. Mayor?" Amusement warred with embarrassment in her eyes.

"We're in the jungle. Good to be wary."

Her eyes snapped to his in a moment of shared understanding. "Can't be too careful of wild animals."

He felt like tearing off her clothes with his teeth, so he knew he'd qualify. Quickly, he turned away. "I'm going to change out of this suit." He pawed through the boxes, pulling out the ones he knew contained clothes for him. "I hope I guessed your size right. If not, I think they'll be close." He headed for the bathroom, already thinking of somewhere else to go. Alone. Away from this too-tempting woman.

As he closed the door behind him, he heard her

speak but couldn't make out the words. With a silent groan, he pulled it back open a crack. "What?"

"I said, you're a good man, Michael Longstreet. An honorable man. If you want, we can share the bed and just make a bolster between us."

"Great." Michael closed the door and leaned back against it. He was supposed to sleep in a bed with her like some damn eunuch? He'd sleep in the car first. His blood could use some cooling.

Honor was a real pain in the behind sometimes. And it did absolutely nothing to satisfy an ache that seemed likely to only get worse with every day they were locked inside this sham marriage.

But at least back in Prosperino they could give each other wide berth. He would concentrate on that and do his best to get through the endless night ahead of them.

# Six

Michael woke up and checked the clock. Four o'clock in the morning. Somehow they'd made it through the evening, thanks to a channel that played old movies. He'd had no idea Suzanne was a black-and-white film buff. *The Maltese Falcon* had been showing, and she'd regaled him with everything she knew about the story behind the production. With every minute that had passed without touching, they'd relaxed a little more. They'd wound up eating the whole pizza, but he'd put the champagne away, fearing to light the powder keg again.

Now something warm on his chest moved, shocking him out of the dream state. He glanced down to where he lay on the covers, fully dressed for safety's sake, and realized it was Suzanne's hand reaching across the bolster he'd decided was an excellent idea, after all. In her sleep, she clutched loosely at his shirt. Heat rippled through his body like lightning.

He closed his eyes again, squeezed them tightly. Breathed through pinched nostrils until he could beat the craving back.

Then he studied the hand, striving for the eyes of an indifferent observer. Yeah, indifferent. Sure thing.

Her hand was so slender, her fingers long and graceful, his ring a gleaming circle that suited her hand well, though he was sure she didn't think so. Short and unpainted, her nails were beautiful but not pampered, much like Suzanne herself. She worked hard, pouring her energies into others rather than herself. She dressed in simple, clean lines, no obvious jewelry, no self-indulgence at all that he'd ever seen.

Too bad. With her stunning coloring, she was more suited to designer frocks than the brown wren clothes she chose. Maybe, while they were together, he could indulge her a little in ways she never would.

But right now he needed distance from her, from the hand that lay so trustingly on his chest. Carefully, he slipped out of the bed. He was resisting her for the moment, but he didn't want to press his luck. He could remember only too easily how craving had dug in its claws before they'd found the blessed distraction of the movie.

He'd discovered, during those hours of enforced civility, that he liked Suzanne. Liked her a lot. If she hadn't been a woman—and so damn beautiful—she could have been a great running buddy.

Liking her helped him gain perspective. Her mind was so agile, her sense of humor unexpected and quirky. She worked hard at a difficult job. She was a generous, caring woman totally focused on trying to regain something she needed badly: her son.

She was passionate, yes, and he knew that sex between them would be explosive. But he'd been right when he said she led with her heart. If he seduced her into bed with him as he badly ached to do, he doubted that she would be able to consider it just sex—and he had nothing more to offer.

He'd walked into this arrangement so blithely, thinking only on the surface. She needed a temporary husband; he needed a temporary wife. Logical. Practical. A simple solution for both of them. She was a big girl; he was a grown man. They'd play their parts in the game for a while and walk away clean, he'd thought.

But he hadn't counted on wanting her like this. Hadn't expected to find the tender underbelly on a woman who'd been such a sharp-tongued adversary. His conscience balked at taking advantage of her passionate nature, no matter how much he wanted to sink in to the luxury of that fine body.

So they would be friends and nothing more. Her

ground rules were smart, and he would follow them to the letter. In time he would get used to her, would be able to ignore the attraction.

And then, one day not far down the road, it would be over. He would be able to walk away easily, knowing he had done the right thing.

For now he would take each step as it came. Carefully, he slipped out the door of the suite to call the airfield, hoping to high heaven that now that the skies were clear he could get them back to the world they knew, back to normal life. Back where he could keep his distance from a woman who appealed to him too much—before he did something foolish that would wreck this precarious peace.

Suzanne stepped down from the plane, noting that Michael kept a careful distance this time as he helped her to the ground. The flight back had been accomplished in virtual silence, punctuated only by an occasional remark on what lay below or how the weather had improved.

Today was one of the rare clear days in Prosperino, not a remnant of fog, only buttery yellow sunshine. Dewdrops still glistened on the trees and grass, and the crisp air held only a slight chill. Suzanne's worry lifted as she looked around.

They would do all right. The turbulence of yesterday had given way to a careful truce between them. This was how it would be, from this day on. She would do everything in her power to keep this fragile peace between them. No matter how he made her heart race.

"Michael?"

He was several steps ahead of her, carrying his suit bag and the sacks from his shopping trip, now filled with her dress and heels. She was wearing the wool pants and sweater he'd bought her, warm boots on her feet, every bit of the clothing far more costly than anything she'd ever bought herself, the quality of workmanship something she'd only dreamed of owning. Perhaps Meredith Colton could help her figure out what value she should put down in the book of expenses she was keeping, despite what Michael had said.

"What?" He barely turned toward her. All morning she'd felt invisible.

"How soon do you think we could go see Bobby?"

He turned, his face impassable. "You don't need to wait for me."

"He needs to meet you. He's going to be living with you, Michael. As your son."

One quick dart of pain flared in his darkening green eyes. A muscle in his jaw ticked, but then he let out a breath and his shoulders settled, though he didn't look happy. "Let's get you moved in first, Suzanne. Let's give ourselves a few days to get used to all these changes."

Oh, no. He didn't want Bobby here. This wasn't

going to work, she knew it in her bones. She should never have done this.

He continued, "It would be dangerous for the pup to roam loose at my place. I'll have to get a fence built, but if I get someone on it right away, maybe we can bring both of them over next weekend."

Relief rushed over her. "You'd do that?"

"The boy's got some rough times ahead of him. Seems to me he'll need his furry friend."

"Yes. He will." She stepped closer, reaching out to touch his arm, to express her gratitude.

He stiffened and started to step away, then glanced back at the building behind him. "Zeb will be inside the terminal. He'll be our first audience. Guess we'd better start making our case for a love match." The reluctance in his voice made it seem impossible.

Yesterday had been a roller coaster, but last night she'd thought they had a shot at becoming friends, at getting through this charade with only minor scratches. But today he was so remote. Not at all the easygoing Michael everyone knew.

"I'm sorry, Michael."

He frowned. "Sorry for what?"

"Sorry that we have to do this. Maybe we should call it quits right now before—"

"No." His jaw went hard as steel. "It's too late for that. You've told Bobby and Jim. I've told my parents. For better or for worse, we're stuck with this."

Stuck. It was foolish, but the word stung. She'd never wanted to make any man feel that way about being with her. Humiliation swept over her.

"Suzanne—"

"Don't." She swallowed hard, fury rushing to her rescue. "Don't you dare pity me. I've made a life for myself without anyone's help, and I won't be a millstone around anyone's neck."

Michael swore harshly. "Come here," he muttered, leading her around the corner of the building, away from the windows.

She jerked her arm away from his grip. "Don't order me around, Michael Longstreet. You're used to getting your way, but your money doesn't buy you any leverage with me."

"Dammit, Suzanne, I don't pity you." Sparks of temper shot from his gaze.

"The devil you don't." Her voice rose. "I'm not poor Suzanne. Get that straight." She poked her finger in his chest. "I'm just as stuck with you as you are with me, and you're no bargain, pretty boy, no matter what your parents may have told you all your life. You're hardheaded and used to getting your own way. You like bossing people around and you think that smile of yours fools everyone, but I'm telling you—" she poked him again "—it doesn't fool me."

He dropped the sacks in one hand and grabbed her hand. "That finger ought to need a permit. It's a lethal weapon."

But he was grinning at her, curse him. Grinning! The sight of it shot her temper out of orbit. "Don't you laugh at me, Rich Boy. Don't you dare." Her voice almost a growl, she struggled to pull her hand from his.

When he laughed, she shoved at his chest.

He dropped his suit bag and pulled her into his arms with breathless speed.

"I said, stop laughing." Her attempts at battle were futile as his strong arms patiently held her.

Furious embarrassment kept her struggling a moment longer, but his arms were too strong. His body too warm. Then his mouth lowered to hers.

Too hot. Too tempting. He angled her head to taste her more deeply.

And then there was only this. Only the kiss. Tiny embers of temper flared in one last futile attempt at resistance, but the power of Michael's kiss turned temper into something dark and sweet.

Suzanne fell headlong into the kiss, pressing her breasts against his muscled chest, her thighs against his. Need swept through her like a brushfire, and reason deserted her utterly.

She heard Michael groan and felt him grip her more tightly, felt him hard and ready against her. She slid her hands into his hair and grabbed on for the ride.

"Well, boy, exactly what do we have here?" a ragged voice cackled.

Suzanne and Michael jumped apart instantly, and she turned around to see the wizened old caretaker who kept Prosperino's tiny airfield running.

Face flaming, trying to adjust to the quick dive from arousal to shame, she tried to step away, but Michael slid one arm around her waist and held her close.

Her heart was pounding and she seemed to have lost the power of speech.

Michael's voice was steady, though, and she tried not to resent it. For Romeo Rich Boy, she supposed this was nothing new, but she felt the bite of disappointment when he grinned so casually and looked so unmoved. "We have a couple on their honeymoon, Zeb. Why don't you just go back where you came from?"

The tiny old man scratched his chin, watery blue eyes bright. "Honeymoon? You? And her?" He pointed to Suzanne. "Ain't she the one who's always yellin' at you at the meetin's?"

When Michael grinned again and winked, she wanted to kick him. "She's a passionate woman, Zeb. What can I say?"

Zeb frowned. "You married her?"

She stiffened and pulled away, but Michael's arm was a steel band around her. "Look at her, Zeb. You get a shot at a filly this prime, wouldn't you want to brand her as your own?" His voice was easy, but he cast a glance of warning at her.

Brand? She'd kill him for sure. Find something heavy and knock him on that thick, arrogant head.

Zeb cackled again and looked over her, then nodded. "'spect I would, boy. 'spect I would."

"If you two Neanderthals would excuse this little filly to go to the ladies' room?" She didn't try to keep the acid from her voice or the sparks from her eyes.

But Michael didn't just let her go. He leaned down and kissed her hard, then whispered against her lips. "Play nice."

She whispered back. "In your dreams." When he chuckled, his arm relaxed and she pulled free. Without a backward glance, she stalked away from them both.

But not quickly enough to miss their next exchange.

"Spirited, isn't she, Zeb?" And damn him, Michael chuckled again.

"Yep. B'lieve you got your hands full, boy, but she's a looker. You'd best keep tight reins on that one."

Spirited. Tight reins. Just wait until she got Michael alone. She'd read him the riot act. Sure they had to pretend, but there were limits to this charade. He made her so mad sometimes, so mad she forgot herself, so mad—

That last kiss flashed into her mind, and she knew the cost of losing her temper. That devastating, curl-your-toes kiss had happened after she'd let fury grab hold.

Her temper had always been fiery and easily aroused. Around Michael, it was lethal. He was easy-going to a point, but he would not be pushed around. And touching him, even in aggravation, could spark the fire between them that never seemed to cool.

For the sake of everyone involved, she'd better keep a much tighter rein on herself. Prime, spirited filly that she was.

As she walked away, she tried in vain to stifle a smile. She didn't want to like Michael Longstreet so much, curse his charming soul.

But it didn't seem to matter.

As they drove into Prosperino, Michael finally spoke. Up till now they'd maintained another careful silence. "How about if I take you to my place first so you see the surroundings and figure out what you'd like to bring over for tonight?"

"Tonight?" She'd been thinking about climbing into her own bed and pulling the covers over her head.

He cast her one quick glance, then continued in a dry tone. "I'm pretty sure newlyweds who elope in the heat of passion are expected to start spending their nights together right away. Would you rather do it at your place?"

She thought about Michael filling up all the space

in her small apartment and decided then and there to keep it for another month, at least, as a refuge. In that case, the less he was there, the better a bolt-hole it would make. "No. You're right. I—I just wasn't thinking." She tried to stem the butterflies suddenly loose in her stomach.

He noticed. "It's not a bad house, I promise." But there was an odd note in his voice.

Maybe he had butterflies, too?

She glanced out the window, mentally shaking her head. Romeo Rich Boy? Hardly.

Soon they were climbing the slope to the mountaintop retreat she'd heard about but never seen. She looked around her, memorizing the route, noticing how the road disappeared around curves into dense forest.

Then suddenly, the road leveled, opening onto a spacious clearing. To the left she saw a barn and pens and—

"Horses." A deep sigh escaped her. She loved horses.

He glanced over. "Do you ride?"

She shrugged. "I'm not great, but I love it. How many do you have?"

"Seven. Probably seven too many, but I'm a soft touch."

"Do you raise them to sell or race or something?"

He chuckled. "Nope. Just to consume staggering amounts of feed and require endless hours of work."

But she could hear the love of them in his voice. "I missed having horses when I was back east." The sorrow she'd heard before was there, an undertone of grief.

"So when I came back, I knew I wanted a place with room enough for a horse."

"But you couldn't stop at one?" she teased.

He nodded ruefully. "People get horses and then can't care for them and want to get rid of them, not always in kind ways." He shrugged his broad shoulders. "The vets in the area seem to have figured out that I'm an easy mark. My place has become the horse foster home for the area."

"So you just keep them for a while until they find good homes?"

Color dusted his cheeks, and she was fascinated by it.

"That was the plan. Unfortunately, I'm pretty picky on what I consider a good home. And then I get attached."

Every time she turned around, she discovered some new, surprising facet to a man she'd once considered unbearably arrogant and hardheaded. The knowledge disturbed her. He'd made it clear that his heart was not available. Caring too much about him would only break her own heart.

"Bobby will love it. Jim used to ride in rodeos and Bobby has inherited his love of horses."

"Does Bobby have his own horse?"

She shook her head. "I don't think so."

Michael slowed and pointed to a paint. "That mare is very gentle and she's not too big. Daisy might be a good match for him."

Gratitude swamped her. She reached out and brushed his arm. "Michael, you're doing so much for him. I don't know if—"

"It's no big deal." His jaw flexed as he shifted away from her touch. "Daisy needs exercise, and I could use the help. If you're interested, pick out the one you want to use while you're here."

While you're here. The words snapped her back into what was real. She and Bobby would only be guests, only for a small span of time. She'd do well to remember that.

He drove on, and she studied the house up ahead. It was like nothing she would have ever expected from the man she'd always considered some kind of misplaced urban sophisticate, despite his boots and jeans.

This, she realized, was more than a house. It looked like home, like the very definition of the word, and she couldn't be more surprised that Michael had chosen it. Two stories and Victorian, it looked big enough to shelter a family, a place where you grew up with traditions and handed them down with love. A dusty blue with darker blue and white trim, it was the jewel in this wonderful, unexpected place, the harbor she'd wished for all of her life.

"It's beautiful, Michael." She turned and caught the quiet pride in his smile.

Michael stopped the car in front of the house and pointed to the left side. "I thought I'd get the pen for the pup built there. That way when nobody's home, he's safe from wandering so far away he gets lost, but he's right next to the house so he'll have shelter. We'll get him a doghouse, too."

"I'll pay for—"

He rounded on her, eyes snapping. "Maybe I'll want a dog when you're gone, ever think of that? Dammit, Suzanne, we're not keeping score here. I can't be wondering every second if I'm spending money that will beggar you."

"You've never had to worry about money, have you?" It was such a novel idea, she couldn't quite take it in.

His shoulders stiffened. "For your information, I once had to count every cent."

"When was that?"

"When I defied my parents and married my wife. They cut me off without a penny. I've never accepted anything from them since. Everything I have, I've made on my own."

She'd always assumed his wealth was inherited, that he was a trust-fund kid. "What a terrible surprise that must have been."

"It wasn't a surprise," he snapped. "I knew they would do it."

"And you went ahead, anyway." She studied him. "You must have loved her very much."

He stared into the distance, his jaw rigid. "My pride cost her everything."

"Why do you say that?"

His head whipped around. In his eyes was a bleakness she'd never seen on a living soul. "I'd call her life everything, wouldn't you? Her life and our baby?"

Then suddenly he was out of the car, leaving the air behind him stinging with an angry grief bigger than she knew how to handle. She wanted to understand. She wanted to go to him, to soothe him, but he'd walked around to grab their things from the back, and every implacable line of his frame shouted out a warning not to trespass.

Something festered deep inside him, but she was a stranger. She had no right to pry into something so obviously painful. If his friends and family hadn't been able to find a way past his guard, how could she expect to do so?

But she still wanted to help, so she opened the car door and emerged, following him up the steps. "Michael, maybe it would be good for you to talk about—"

His hand stilled on the screen door. Slowly, very slowly, he turned. His face was the mask of a stranger, a hard man she didn't want to know. "Suzanne, get one thing straight. This marriage is a charade we will act out for the benefit of others. I will do my best to get along with you and your son and make this time as comfortable as possible for all of us.''

Then his voice lost its careful neutrality. ''But if you want to stay in this house past the next second, you will never, ever ask me about my wife and son again.'' The green eyes that could be soft and warm and funny were hard as malachite now. ''Is that clear?''

She felt like nothing so much as a chastened child. If she hadn't heard the enormous relief in Jim's voice that she would be able to take Bobby, she'd turn around right now and walk back to town, right after telling Michael Longstreet to go straight to hell.

But her son and the good man who loved him were depending on her. So she clenched her jaw and bit out the words. ''Very clear.''

''Fine.'' He held the door open for her. ''After you.''

''Fine.'' She swept ahead of him in high dudgeon, not sparing a glance for her surroundings. ''If you'll show me my room, I'll take a look and then you can take me home.''

He didn't try to mouth any platitudes about this being her new home. It was abundantly clear now that this would never be more than a way station. She would check first thing Monday morning on getting someone else to help her with gaining legal custody of Bobby. She would bite her tongue off before she asked this man for the tiniest favor that wasn't absolutely required by this sham of a marriage.

She followed him upstairs, mentally making a list of all she'd need to do to get this over with as soon as possible. When Michael stopped at a doorway, she almost plowed right into him.

He stepped aside and gestured. "Here it is. Bobby will be over there." He pointed to a room diagonally across the landing.

She didn't ask where he would be. In the barn would suit her fine. Then she stepped into the room and almost gasped with pleasure.

It was a woman's room, that was obvious. A stunning mahogany four-poster bed was set diagonally in the far corner, its coverlet a pale lavender satin. Fluffy, lacy pillows were mounded at the head. Gleaming oak floors were topped with a beautiful rug in pale cream, mint green and all shades of lavender and rose. An antique vanity with a big rounded mirror stood against the wall nearest the door, and in the corner to her left, a chaise angled by the window, a place to read and dream.

She'd never seen a more beautiful room in her life. Then an uneasy suspicion grew. "You shouldn't have gone to all this trouble."

"I didn't. The former owners sold it to me fully furnished. I've remodeled and replaced some things in the spaces I use most, but I left this room as it was. I don't know why.''

He sounded almost embarrassed, and some of the hurt leaked out of her.

*Be an adult, Suzanne. He has a right to his secrets.*

She was about to turn around, an apology on her lips, when she spotted the door just before the chaise and walked to it, pulling it open, expecting a closet.

What she found was far too big to be called simply a closet. To her left, she spotted racks of men's clothing and shelves filled with shoes and other decidedly male gear. To her right were empty racks and shelves. ''What is this?'' Before he could answer, she spotted a door across from her and was almost certain she knew.

''It's a dressing room,'' he answered.

But she hadn't read a million historical romances for nothing. She whirled and pointed a finger at him. ''Don't tell me your bedroom is through that door.''

His eyes went flat. ''All right. I won't tell you.''

''Michael, this won't work. Give me another room.''

''There isn't another room.''

''Give me Bobby's room.''

''A ten-year-old boy would hate this room. It would attack his very tenuous manhood.''

''Then use some of that money you're so free with and redecorate it for him.''

"What am I supposed to do with all these furnishings? They won't fit in the other room."

She tried not to feel the pang of loss over a room she already adored. "I don't care. Store them or whatever."

"No."

"No? Just like that, no?"

"If you want it, you pay for it."

She sucked in a breath. "You know I can't afford that. It would cost a fortune."

"Exactly."

"You could do it, Michael."

He shrugged. "But I don't want to."

"I can't believe you're behaving like this."

His cold eyes challenged her. "Are you saying you can't resist me? That you don't have the self-control to stay in your own room?"

"Of course not," she snapped. "It's just—"

"There are two doors between us. You can shove a chair under the knob if you think your charm is so fatal that my self-control will fail."

She thought of hot, deep kisses and his hard male body pressing into hers—but then she reminded herself that she'd just seen a side of him she hadn't known. That he could be hard and cold, that he'd just demonstrated vividly how unsuitable she'd always known they were.

This man had women aplenty only too happy to

fall into his arms. Women who were hothouse flowers, not sturdy weeds.

"Fine. But you knock before you enter the dressing room, and I'll do the same."

He quickly shuttered his gaze and nodded. Walking to the bed, he laid her packages on the coverlet. "I'll be downstairs whenever you're ready to leave. Look around all you want. I have no secrets."

She watched him go, mouth agape at the blatant falsehood. Maybe he really believed that, but she knew she'd never met a more complicated or mystifying man in her life.

She started to follow him down, then decided a break was in order. A few minutes apart, after the intensity of the last two days, would be very welcome.

She should go see what Bobby's room looked like. It still didn't seem real that someday soon her child would live with her, that she would be the mother she'd wanted to be for ten years. Fear set down roots in her chest, a fear she'd been keeping at bay until now, caught up in the whirlwind of this marriage.

She'd dealt with kids for years and had been good with them, but being a mother was completely different. What if she couldn't give Bobby everything he needed? What if he and Michael didn't suit? Worse, what if he got attached to Michael?

Fear was a hammer tattooing a beat on her heart. Nothing had ever meant more in her life than doing this right, than reclaiming the child she'd never wanted to give up. She could still recall his tiny features, the perfect shell of his ears, the nose smaller than a button, the dark hair so like hers that lay against his fragile skull. She'd only had a few moments with him, and she'd spent too many of them wanting to take back her promise, to forget everything she'd known was best for him.

Drying up the milk in her breasts had been painful, but it had paled against the agony of drying up the love in her heart. The best she'd been able to do was to lock down the forbidden chamber where yearning for her child still dwelled to this day. She'd done the right thing for Bobby because she'd been too young, had had no resources to care for him the way he deserved.

But knowing that had never seemed to lessen the pain. The best she'd been able to do was to transfer that need to the children she tried to help.

Which brought the children of Hopechest Ranch to mind. Time to stop thinking about this marriage and its dilemmas and get back to work. She couldn't see Bobby until the weekend, but these kids needed her now. With quick steps, she crossed the landing and opened the door, eager to get a quick peek and get back to work.

Bobby's room was smaller, but it was in a corner with two sets of windows that gave him a wonderful view of the horses, the barn, and the area where Michael would build Maverick an enclosure. The furnishings were simple, and the walls mostly bare. She liked that. It meant Bobby could put his stamp on the room, if Michael were willing, and that she could provide some things, at last, for her own child.

Satisfied, she closed the door, then moved down the hall and opened the next room, which turned out to be a basic hall bath, nothing fancy. Updated since the house's Victorian roots, but still with nice touches like the pedestal sink and clawfoot tub with shower. A little crowded for all of them to use, but they could make do. It still dwarfed the tiny bathroom in her apartment.

The final door on that side opened to what had once been a bedroom but was clearly Michael's home office. Sleek laptop computer, a color printer and fax combined. Lots of shelves filled with books surrounded a huge cherry partner's desk covered with papers. She'd like to look at the books on his shelves to learn more about him, but she'd have to get too near his papers, and despite what he'd said, it seemed an invasion of his privacy. She closed that door and headed for the stairs.

Her hand paused on the rounded newel post, and she glanced at the door she now knew led to Michael's bedroom. Part of her was unbearably tempted to peek, but most of her shied away. She had no reason to see Michael's bedroom, and the more distance they kept between them, the better. He'd made his need for that distance very, very clear.

So Suzanne ignored the insatiable curiosity that had always been a part of her and instead set her feet heading back downstairs. It would not be an easy balance, making this place feel like home for Bobby when she knew it was only a way station on a journey to their future. If cousin Edna would only give up her claim to Bobby, Suzanne would dispense with this charade before she ever had to move Bobby in and avoid the potential confusion that now seemed to lurk in every corner.

But Jim had made it clear when she'd called that he could only hope this marriage would placate Edna, that he was certain she would be watching Suzanne like a hawk for some time to come.

So there was no choice for Suzanne but to set her mind to making a success of this very complicated venture. For the foreseeable future, she had to forget about the day it would all be over and concentrate on finding a way to live in peace and harmony with a man who preferred to be alone. To make a marriage in name only appear real. To be certain that the child who owned her heart got plenty of love from her so that when Michael and she were free to call it quits, her son would suffer as little as possible.

Suzanne realized that she should be very, very grateful that Michael himself had no wish to be more than a kind, distant friend to her son. It was the best thing for all of them. Logic said that the worst thing she could do would be to yield to the inexplicably powerful physical reaction between her and Michael. It would be unfair and stupid and even dangerous. Her tendency to let emotion triumph over logic was her worst enemy right now, and beating the enemy had never been more important. She was locked in a battle for her son and could not afford a single mistake.

She reached the bottom step and spotted Michael on the telephone in the kitchen, looking out the window. Looking too good.

She'd made a lot of mistakes in her life, but she feared, deep in her bones, that she would never find one bigger—or more tempting—than getting too close to Michael Longstreet.

# Seven

Michael listened to Blake Fallon finish detailing what had been done yesterday to set up today's move of the kids from Hopechest Ranch to the Colton estate. A day early.

"Sounds like it's going smoothly, all things considered."

"Yeah," Blake said. "Considering you stole my right arm. How is Suzanne?" He paused for a moment, obviously waiting for an explanation.

"Suzanne?" Second thoughts bombarded Michael.

Then Blake laughed. "Surely you two don't think you can keep this secret. Zeb was on the phone two seconds after you left. The circuits are melting from

overload. What the devil's going on, buddy? You and
*Suzanne?*''

Michael whirled away from the window and started
to pace. The next few seconds would be critical, and
he needed to be a better actor. Maybe she was right,
maybe they should just forget—

Movement in the doorway caught his eye. Suzanne
stood there, her eyes no longer angry, only confused.

Now or never, buddy. Fish or cut bait.

"Hey, Longstreet, you still there? I was sure Zeb
was imagining things. You and Suzanne can't be in
the same room for five minutes without arguing. But
then I went to breakfast this morning and Ruby told
me you laid quite a kiss on Suzanne Friday night. You
been drinking the water at the ranch and lost your
mind or what?"

Michael didn't look away from Suzanne for another moment, caught by indecision. She looked so
small and delicate. So alone. She held his gaze, waiting to see what he would do.

He sucked in a deep breath and ran one hand over
his hair, gripping the back of his neck. "What can I
say, Blake? The sparks that have been flying for
months finally caught fire."

Blake whistled. "You're serious? Zeb isn't making
it up?"

Suzanne's eyes closed quickly, then opened again,
warm with gratitude.

He shot her a rueful smile and shrugged. "Zeb's

not making it up. We got married in Tahoe yester-day.''

''Holy smokes! Michael, you don't have to marry a woman to take her to bed. Suzanne's hot all right, but—''

''Careful, Blake.'' Though he would have agreed with the sentiment about sex and marriage before, he balked at anyone talking about Suzanne like that, even his good friend. ''We've been striking sparks off each other for a long time. It just took me awhile to figure out why. We've been spending some time together and finally I realized that she's what's been missing in my life.'' He wished he didn't have an audience in the room, Lying to his friend while Suzanne listened was hard to swallow.

But Blake had to be convinced. If he weren't, no one else would buy it.

''It's awful damn sudden, man. Are you sure about this?''

''Suzanne's not the type to have an affair.'' That, at least, he could say with total conviction.

''But marriage?''

''I know it seems sudden, but we just…knew. I've never felt like this, Blake.'' It was true, but not in the way he hoped Blake would take it.

''You get a prenup?''

Damn, this just kept getting more complicated. ''No,'' he gritted out. ''I'm not worried about my money and no one else should be, either. She's not like that.'' Another truth to mix in with all the lies.

''Hey, you don't have to convince me of that. I know Suzanne, probably better than you. She's first-class all the way. I was just wondering what your folks would think.''

''My parents are fine with it.'' Actually, they were as shocked as Blake, but since it fell in line with their fondest wish, they were adjusting surprisingly well. But he didn't want to talk about this anymore. ''We just got back and Suzanne's been itching to find out about the kids. Here she is.'' With that, he handed her the phone—and the hot potato topic.

She hesitated, then took the phone as if he'd handed her a lit stick of dynamite. ''Blake? How are the kids? I thought we weren't moving them until Monday or I'd never have—''

Michael watched her pace the floor, one hand fidgeting with the ends of her hair as she asked about one child and then another, the depth of her caring obvious.

''I'll get Michael to take me to get my car and I'll be right out there—'' She fell silent as Blake interrupted. ''Honeymoon?'' Her face went blank for a second, then she shot Michael a look. ''No, uh, we know we can't possibly take one right now, not with all that's going on.'' When Michael nodded, she continued. ''He and I agreed to wait until all this is over. The town needs him and the kids need me.''

After another pause, she smiled fondly. "We'll be fine. We're both adults, Blake, not kids. We have responsibilities that must be taken care of. We wouldn't have been gone overnight except that we got snowed in." She chewed at her lower lip while Blake said something else, then laughter burst out. "No, I don't think Michael's rich enough to control the weather. Even Joe Colton couldn't pull that off. And anyway, I'm not exactly a femme fatale."

That's what you think. Michael frowned at the certainty in her voice. What did the woman see when she looked in the mirror? Was she blind? They might have severe differences in philosophy and emotional needs, but surely she hadn't missed what she did to him physically. All things being equal, he'd keep her naked and in his bed for the next decade.

But all things weren't equal and never would be.

Suzanne's cheeks flared with hectic color as she told Blake good-bye and hit the disconnect button. For all her boldness and fire, there was an aspect of her that was almost virginal, never mind that he knew she'd had a child at sixteen. She was a complicated woman, entirely too fascinating for his peace of mind.

"Well," she said on an exhale. "That was awkward."

He had to chuckle. "Very." He blew out his own gust of air, settling his hands on his hips. "And it won't be the last conversation like that we have to negotiate. Let's just hope the small-town grapevine does its job and people get tired of the novelty quickly.''

Mischief played around her lips. "I could almost be grateful for the water crisis. Otherwise, we'd be the only game in town."

He met her smile with one of his own, shuddering for effect. "Don't. You'll give me nightmares."

They shared a small laugh that died away quickly, leaving strain in its wake.

"Look, I'm sorry about—" He shrugged and nodded toward the stairs. "I knew it would be awkward, but it's a nice room and I thought you'd be comfortable there. I can get a lock put on, so you don't have to worry about—"

She waved his concern away. "No. I won't worry. It's just...difficult. But no more difficult for me than for you, having your solitude vanish like this." She glanced around. The kitchen was state-of-the-art but not cold. "It's a lovely home, Michael. I can see the improvements you've made, but you've kept the essential character of this beautiful old house. And Bobby's room is perfect because it's got places where he can make it his. We'll do our best to stay out of your way, though I'll apologize right now because I don't think our best will be good enough."

He shook his head. "It'll be fine. Sometimes this place is awfully big for one person. The house will probably enjoy the feeling of a family again—even an imposter family. The family who built it had six children. These old walls may be tired of all the silence." Looking at her, he held out a hand. "Truce?"

She smiled and extended her own. "Truce. And thank you."

When their hands touched, he felt that special jolt only Suzanne's skin conveyed to his, but he studiously ignored it. "I thought I'd take you to meet my parents this evening. You up for that?"

Her hand pulled away, her eyes going wide. "Oh, Michael, I told Blake I'd be right out there." She exhaled in a gust. "And truth to tell, I'm not ready. I know you have things to do and I have to head for the ranch. Do you think they'd understand if we did it tomorrow?"

"I'd call you a coward, but I feel the same way."

"They won't like me, will they?" Her voice went flat.

"No, that's not it. They'll like you fine. They'll be thrilled. It's just...the acting part is wearing."

"You're not kidding. I didn't know how hard it would be."

He knew it shouldn't bother him to know that she found it hard to pretend to be crazy about him, but it did sting, more than he wanted to admit. *You're no bargain, pretty boy.* A chuckle escaped him.

"What?" she asked.

"Nothing. Just...this whole thing." He glanced up at her, not even vaguely ready to explain. "I'll call my folks. They understand about duty—it's their favorite word to me, so I'll just turn it on them. So, you ready to head back to town?''

She nodded. ''Ready as I'll ever be, I guess. I wouldn't mind some Groucho glasses at the moment, though.''

He chuckled and gestured for her to proceed him. ''If you find some, buy two sets.''

When Suzanne's musical laughter danced over his hearing, Michael decided the only way to handle this was one minute at a time. They'd passed another hurdle, and that had to count for something.

Suzanne pulled into the gates of Hopechest Ranch and saw a beehive of activity, cars and pickups and vans parked everywhere while the kids milled around carrying a hodgepodge of belongings from stuffed animals to boomboxes.

She should have been there for them, not off on some crazy trek with Michael. These kids had been her life for the last year, and she'd let them down. Never mind that Blake had ordered her to take the weekend off because the move wouldn't come until Monday. For whatever reason, the move was happening on Sunday instead, and she should have been here.

Still castigating herself, she emerged from the car. With a loud cry, a heavily pregnant teenager launched herself toward Suzanne.

"Suzanne, we have to leave!" Joetta Pearsall moved close, and Suzanne tucked her under one arm.

"I know, honey. But you'll be all right. I—" She was all prepared to launch into an apology, when Joetta went on.

"It's awesome. We get to stay at the Colton ranch," she chattered. Suzanne realized that the girl's eyes were bright with anticipation, not fear. "And Mrs. Colton—she told us to call her Meredith—she says that we're going to make it like a big slumber party. I've never been to a slumber party," the sixteen-year-old confided. "But Cathy and Jennifer and Linda and Vickie all think it's the ench."

Suzanne was conversant enough in teenspeak to know that "the ench" was short for "the big enchilada"—their way of indicating that something was beyond cool, a dated word they'd die before uttering. Faced with Joetta's elation, Suzanne felt something inside her ease a bit. If her pregnant charges were viewing this as a big adventure, that was one big worry off her list.

And she had to admit, a slumber party with glamorous Meredith Colton would have made her own teenage heart race.

"I'm absolutely certain that Meredith will show you a time like you've never seen before." She hugged Joetta's slender shoulders and pressed a kiss to her hair. "So you're feeling okay, honey?"

"Oh yeah, but boy, am I looking forward to taking

a really long shower. Taking these sponge baths is getting old.''

Since the day that the cause of the sickness sweeping Hopechest Ranch had been discovered, Blake had been trucking water in, but a ranch with this many teenagers—and their propensity for long, hot showers—couldn't keep up with the demand. The first thing to go had been the showers.

"I hear you." Despite the whirlpool last night, Suzanne found herself craving a long shower where she didn't have to worry about Michael's presence. As soon as the kids were all safely delivered and settled in, she fully intended to take one of her own before she packed.

"Hey, Ms. Jorgenson," said Maria Delgado, a new and very shy resident of Emily's House.

"Hello, Maria." Suzanne reached out to hug the girl to her other side. Soon, several kids were gathered round, eagerly chatting about the new break in their routine. She relaxed as she realized that all of them seemed far more thrilled about living at the palatial Hacienda de Alegria than worried about the change. She should have taken into account a teenager's love of a new thrill.

"Hey, Ms. Jorgenson, we'll be moving the animals, too, and—"

"Suzanne, do you know that the Colton ranch has—"

"Mr. Colton said we could—"

A babel of voices surrounded her. She drank in every second of it, the uncertainties of her private life fading as she concentrated on these kids who were far more than a job to her.

Then Blake Fallon walked up, his eyes twinkling. "Ms. Jorgenson had an interesting weekend of her own. Anything you'd like to share?" He winked, enjoying himself hugely.

Suzanne realized that Blake was only the first of many who would have fun over what she and Michael had done. Blake's tone made it clear that he'd bought into Michael's version that they'd been swept away by passion.

She felt the rush of heat up her throat and over her cheeks. But she couldn't avoid this. The kids would be hurt to be left out, and they would find out very soon.

"I—" She cleared her throat. "Well, I—" She glanced around at the faces staring at her with great interest. For a moment, she wondered again how she and Michael had ever deluded themselves that they could pull this off as a love match.

But then Bobby's sweet face rose before her. If she didn't pull this off, she would lose him, and that was unthinkable. And he would be meeting these people. This would be his town, unless she and Michael botched things so badly that she had to leave. All that could matter was Bobby's welfare. He would be facing enough in the days to come. She couldn't fail him.

She drew in a deep breath and faced the music. "I got married yesterday. To Michael Longstreet."

For a second, there was a pause loaded with shock. An audible collective indrawn breath.

Then the melee began. "Married?"

"The mayor! No way."

"Wow, Ms. Jorgen—Ms. Longstreet."

"Man, you guys move fast."

She glanced up to see Blake's grin, his slow wink of reassurance. All she could do was wait for the furore to die down. And grin. And shrug. "It's true."

"So what happened to the honeymoon?" One male voice asked—and his voice cracked.

Around him, companionable jeers broke out.

To take the heat off the boy, Suzanne spoke up. "Mr. Longstreet and I will have to wait on the honeymoon." She started to bring up Bobby, but decided that she'd surprised everyone enough for one day. "He's needed until we're sure Prosperino's safe, and I have to make sure you guys stay in line, don't I?"

One breathy girl's voice intervened. "I'd blow us off in a heartbeat, Ms. Jor—Longstreet. The mayor's a babe."

Laughter and feminine nods greeted the statement. Suzanne wanted to slough off the statement. The last thing she needed was to think of Michael's physical appeal. But if this marriage were real, she'd be agreeing with the girl wholeheartedly, so she stayed in character. "He is a babe, Lisa, I can't disagree. But duty calls both of us."

"So will he come with you to visit us more often?" Joetta asked eagerly. "I think he's the ench."

Suzanne had to smile at that. "I'm sure he'd appreciate that, Joetta. He's got a lot on his mind, but I'll see what I can do."

"Okay, gang," Blake intervened. "Time to load up. Suzanne, you don't need to come with us. I think we have enough cars to carry everyone. I'm sure the *ench* would like to have you back as soon as possible." Over the heads of several kids, he winked again, and she knew Michael would be hearing about this even if she never told him.

She stuck out her tongue. "Michael's checking in at city hall. He knows I have a job to do." She turned to Joetta. "Would some of you girls like to ride with me?"

A clamor of voices erupted around her, and Suzanne took welcome refuge in the details of the job that, until yesterday, had been all-consuming.

Michael drove toward Suzanne's apartment hours later, but his mind was not on the help he hoped to offer her with her belongings. His last conversation with the FBI was very much center stage.

The agent had been reticent with real information, but he had told Michael that they were closing in on the source of the contamination at Hopechest Ranch.

Michael wished Rory Sinclair hadn't gone to D.C. to close up his apartment; Sinclair, as a friend of Blake's, would shoot straight with him. Reading between the lines, however, Michael had the distinct impression that the contamination was no accident.

Who would want to poison a ranch full of kids, even troubled kids? Even Homer Wentworth, crabby and disapproving of the Hopechest project as he was, would not do something like that. It was inconceivable that anyone he knew in Prosperino would do such a heinous thing. The world outside might have gotten ugly and edgy, but one beauty of Prosperino had always been its sense of community.

But if no one here had done it, that meant some outside interest intended harm to the ranch.

And maybe to the town, because the same aquifer supplied both town and ranch. From what Michael could gather from talking to an EPA hydrologist, the aquifer ran through limestone and narrowed in many places between the ranch and town so that flow was slow, but eventually whatever had contaminated the ranch well would hit the water supply of Prosperino.

The scientists couldn't speculate with any degree of certainty how soon the town supply could be hit, nor could they predict how much it would be diluted. And no one knew yet how to clean it up, though Joe Colton had spared no expense to bring in experts from around the world.

So for the time being, all that could be done was

to monitor all the wells between the ranch and the town—and wait. And try to keep the citizens calm, which was Michael's job.

Lucky for him, nothing serious had happened while he was stuck in Tahoe overnight. But he would keep himself on a short leash from here on out, no matter how that battled with the need to put together some sort of truce with Suzanne, in addition to all the adjustments that would need to be made for her son.

How he would fit into all this the party his parents were determined to throw later this week to celebrate his marriage, he didn't know. He'd tried to talk them out of it, citing the water emergency, but they'd pointed out that they could easily afford bottled water for everyone and would have the food flown in from San Francisco, if need be.

He could counter those arguments and would have, had he not seen the light of hope in his father's eyes. John Longstreet had stood straighter than Michael had seen him in a while, albeit with great effort. He'd held out his hand, the shimmer of moisture in his eyes, and he'd asked Michael's forgiveness for denying him approval of his marriage to Elaine.

While silent tears rolled down his wife's cheeks, Michael's dad had promised to support his marriage to Suzanne fully and to defend the suddenness of it to any and all comers.

The man who'd squeezed Michael's hand tightly had resembled the father Michael had once known, a vibrant man he'd missed for a very long time. It was as if years had rolled off John Longstreet's shoulders, and Michael could not deny them their party, no matter that the timing couldn't be worse for him.

He pulled into the empty parking space below Suzanne's garage apartment. Pocketing the keys to his Explorer, he took the stairs two at a time while he tried to compose an argument that really only made sense if you cared about his parents, which Suzanne had no reason to do. One more in a line of delicate negotiations that made up this oddball arrangement of theirs.

"Come in," her voice rang out at his knock.

Michael pushed open the door and almost fell over a jungle of potted plants.

"Oh, sorry. I didn't expect you." Suzanne glanced up at him, then turned away to the box she was packing.

An odd relief swept through him at the realization that she was packing as though she meant to stay for some time. He'd half expected to arrive and find that she'd only packed for one night, after all the rough edges between them.

He slid his hands into the back pockets of his jeans. "I thought you might need a hand." Glancing around, he couldn't help smiling. "You got a moving van reserved?"

"I guess I hadn't realized how many—" She gestured around her. "My plants need daily care."

He hadn't understood how much the homey feel he'd registered before had been due to the sheer number of plants she'd managed to load into this apartment. "All these were in the living room?"

Bright spots flared in her cheeks. "No, my bedroom had quite a few, along with the kitchen." Her eyes were laughing as she looked up. "I'm sorry to tell you that this still isn't all of them. I guess I could get rid—"

"No," he interrupted. "We'll find room for all of them." He glanced around dubiously. "Somewhere."

Suzanne laughed the husky laughter of days when things between them weren't so strained. "Good thing it's a big house, huh?"

He grinned back. "Might have to add on."

Her smile faded, as did his. They both knew she'd be gone long before any room could be added.

"Well…" She brushed her hands on the jeans into which she'd changed. "I guess you have everything a kitchen needs."

He shrugged. "I've got the basics. If you need something from yours, maybe it could wait until the next trip." He looked around them again. "I think we've got two vehicles full here, easy."

"Michael, I—" She rubbed her hands over well-worn denim again, drawing Michael's attention back to her legs. "Are you absolutely sure—"

He jerked his gaze away from her slender thighs and a lovely curve of hip. "If your day's been like mine, there's not a soul in this town who doesn't know what we did. I think it's a little late to take it back, don't you?''

She gave him a wry smile. ''It's also too early to be saying 'April Fool,' I guess.'' Then she grinned. ''The girls at the ranch were impressed. It's the consensus that you're the ench.''

He frowned. ''The what?''

Suzanne laughed then, free and easy, and he itched to press his mouth to her throat. But even more than he wanted to do that, he wanted to hear her keep laughing. There was hope for them in that laugh. Hope they would make it through this in one piece.

''The ench. The big enchilada. In teenspeak, it means the girls think you're a hunk. My stock has risen with them, catching Mr. Mayor the Hunk.''

Michael would have bet his last dollar he'd lost the ability to blush by the age of ten, but he didn't need a mirror to know that his cheeks were red. ''Well, I guess that's better than Homer Wentworth asking me what kind of black magic you're practicing, to make me do something so 'goldarn foolish.'''

Faint hurt crossed her features, quickly smothered.

He stepped over two large pots to get near her. ''I told him if he wasn't such a blind fool, he'd see that you were the foolish one, taking up with a scumbag lawyer like he's always calling me.''

Amusement chased away hurt in her eyes. ''That was nice of you.''

"He's a pathetic, embittered old man." He itched to touch her, to soothe her. But he didn't dare. "Ruby says I'd better treat you right so when you come to your senses, you won't run away. And Harmon Atkin says if he'd have known you were that easy to please, he'd have offered himself months ago." Harmon was seventy-five if he was a day.

Suzanne chuckled. "Did you get the sort of speculative looks I've been dodging all day? Those cat-in-cream kind of looks that mean they really want to ask if the sex was that hot?"

He rocked back on his heels, glad to see her easy demeanor again. "Only about a hundred of them. I just smile a lot, so it'll drive them crazy wanting details."

"You're bad." Her voice went husky again, straight to his groin.

"Just giving the folks what they expect," he murmured. He leaned toward her just a fraction, tempted unbearably to kiss those lips that drove him crazy.

Her eyes went wide and for a moment, she stood very still as if she'd welcome it.

Then suddenly she turned away. "Uh, I—I guess I'd better finish packing." With rapid strides, she headed for the bedroom.

He stood in the middle of her tiny living room and sucked in a very deep breath, reminding himself of everything that stood between them and all the dangerous ground they still had to negotiate. They could do it as friends, but becoming lovers would only make a hash of things.

"You're off the hook for seeing my parents tonight or tomorrow, but there's a catch."

"What is it?"

"They want to give us a party Friday night," he called out. Thinking about his parents would cool his blood if anything could.

She shot out of the doorway, her face draining of all color. "A party?"

"A substitute for a wedding reception. They'd like to introduce you to their friends and vice versa. They're talking catering it from San Francisco and inviting friends from all over."

The minute he said it, he knew it was a mistake.

"That would cost a fortune."

"Suzanne," he said tiredly. "It's their money. They want to make you feel welcome."

"I don't need a party."

"You don't have to need it. They do. A lot."

Her jaw jutted mutinously. "But I can't—"

Suddenly he saw the fear behind the resistance. "Don't be afraid. It'll be fun. I swear they don't bite. They—" This was hard for him to talk about. "They never met Elaine. They've never forgiven themselves for the way it turned out. If you could find it in your heart to accept this gesture, it would mean the world to them." He paused for a moment. "It would be a kindness to me, Suzanne."

She glanced down at the sweater gripped in her white-knuckled fingers. "I'm not trying to be a problem. I just—" She lifted her head proudly, swallowing visibly. "I've never been around people like them, Michael."

"People like what?"

"Rich people. Society people. The only time was when the parents of Bobby's father called me to their home and offered me money to go away and not ruin his life." She lifted her gaze to his. "I don't know how to live in that world. I'd embarrass you."

He was deeply touched by her admission and what making it had no doubt cost her. He covered the distance between them and took her hands in his. "You couldn't embarrass me, Suzanne. You're a bright and lovely woman with enormous compassion and a dignity that comes from the bone. I would be proud to have you by my side at that party, and if it would help, I won't leave you the entire night." He met her gaze squarely. "I'm not making this up, I promise. You would be doing me a big favor to agree to this. I'll make it as easy on you as I can, and I promise you my parents will go out of their way, too. This means a lot to them. I'll figure out some explanation if you really can't bring yourself to do it, but I'd be very grateful if you would."

When she didn't answer, he upped the ante. "I'll take you to see Bobby tomorrow, if you'd like."

Her eyes narrowed. He could almost see her back

arch. "I don't need bribing, Michael. And I can take myself to see my son." The insult to her sensibilities almost banished the fear. Almost.

It was funny to him that this same woman who would take on huge government bureaucracies and fight like a wildcat for the kids under her care would be so unnerved by a simple party. Still, he meant what he said. If she really couldn't bring herself to do it, he'd figure out some way to explain it to his parents.

She stared off past his shoulder for a long moment. Then, as if emerging from a dream state, she drew in a long, deep breath and met his gaze squarely. Nerves still danced in her eyes, but courage was there, too. "All right," she answered. "You're doing so much for Bobby. It would be churlish of me to refuse."

If Michael felt a small disappointment that he would never know now if she would have done it but for a sense of debt, he dismissed it. It would be foolish in the extreme to hope that she would go to the party for any other reason than their very practical, very cut-and-dried business arrangement. Tit for tat, that was all this was. All he could expect.

All he wanted.

But the courage she'd shown in face of her terror still moved him. He tapped one finger lightly on her nose. "I swear I'll stay with you until you feel at ease."

Something of the saucy Suzanne flared back. "Then you'd better wear comfortable shoes, Michael

Longstreet. You're going to be standing by me all night."

Between them, laughter eased away a little more of the strain, and Michael took heart from that.

"Okay, let's get this jungle into the cars." He turned to gather up the two biggest pots.

"If only we had a 30-channel remote control sound system to take along."

Michael turned, and between them spun a web of memory and shared laughter.

He'd learned long ago that crying did nothing, but laughter could smooth the path. "Let's go home, Suzanne."

The swift, poignant look that crossed her face just then was something he would ponder far into the night.

# Eight

As they neared Jim Roper's home, Suzanne watched the way Michael drove, one hand draped casually over the top of the steering wheel, his whole big body loose but still with that air of command that came so naturally to him. His was a strong profile, the sort you'd find on a Roman coin, which made the flash of boyish dimples all the more intriguing for their contrast. But that was Michael, she was discovering. A man of contrasts.

She turned back to the needlepoint in her lap, concentrating on the Dallas Cowboys logo for the pillow she would make for Bobby, a diehard fan.

"I can't get over you doing needlepoint," Michael said.

"Why is that?"

"I think of needlepoint in connection with my mom. Something ladies with a lot of time on their hands do." He glanced over. "No wonder you're so skinny. You're never still, are you?" But his mossy green eyes were fond.

She wanted to capture that fondness, that friendly approval. He was chiding her, but he was doing it as a close friend does. Fondness would get them through this. Fondness would protect her son.

To keep from disturbing the fragile peace that, for once, wasn't rippling from the strong physical pull between them, she kept her tone light. "I have a short attention span."

He chuckled. "No, you don't. You've got the persistence of a pit-bull dog. I've prayed for your attention to be distracted more than once, so you'd get off my case." He glanced over. "No pun intended, but that dog won't hunt. You just don't know how to relax, is what I think."

"And you do?"

His lazy smile promised all manner of delights. "I sure do." But he seemed inclined to honor the truce, as well, grinning at her as he said, "Stick with me, kid. I'll show you all about the laid-back life."

She smiled back, thinking that for a man who professed to be lazy, he sure had his fingers in a lot of pies. Then she noticed where they were. "Turn left here. It's about a half mile down on the right."

Inside her, the nerves that had never gone completely silent stirred to life. Since the day, not that long ago, when she'd met her son again, she'd always had a sense of being the intruder, no matter how Jim and Bobby welcomed her. They had a full life here, had a history. Bobby didn't know she was his mother. As far as he was concerned, the only mother he'd ever known had died.

Someday soon he would have to know. Someday soon he would live with her. What if he and Michael didn't suit? What if Bobby hated living with her? What if she couldn't smooth the very rough road ahead for him?

The car stopped. A large warm hand touched hers and squeezed. "Relax. I can hear your brain clicking. It'll be all right."

She looked at Michael's hand on hers. She couldn't remember the last time she'd had anyone to lean on. Dangerous as it was, she soaked in the feeling. After a deep breath, she turned and looked at him. "Thanks."

Then the screen door burst open, and a black dog and a black-haired boy tumbled out. It was time to step out of the car, ready or not.

"Suzanne! Dad got me a dog! Isn't he great?"

The pup raced toward her, slamming into her legs before leaping back, whirling and barking with joy. Suzanne grasped for balance, and Michael was there. She shot him a thankful glance, then leaned down, feeling oddly shy as she ruffled the pup's fur. "He is great. Aren't you, baby? Ooh, you're such a love," she crooned.

The dog slurped a happy kiss up her cheek.

Suzanne laughed. "Oh, you're a heartbreaker."

"His name's Maverick," Bobby offered, but he kept glancing at Michael.

She straightened. "Bobby, this is my husband, Michael Longstreet." How strange it felt to say that word. Husband.

Jim must have prepared Bobby. Without a blink, he stepped forward, holding out his hand as though he were far older than just shy of ten. "Hello, Mr. Longstreet."

"Glad to meet you, Bobby. Suzanne's told me a lot about you." Solemnly, not as one talked to a child, Michael shook his hand and kept his tone adult.

"Yeah? Like what?"

"I hear you like horses."

His eyes, so like her own, widened. "Oh, yes sir. I do. Dad wanted to get me one, but—" He shrugged. The knowledge of Jim's illness suddenly filled the air.

Michael squatted down and wrestled with the pup. "I have horses at my place, too many for me to ride." He kept his tone casual. "Maybe you could help me work them when you come to visit."

Bobby's eyes were the size of dinner plates. "Oh wow, that would be—" Then he broke off, casting a quick glance at the porch. "Well, my dad might need me."

Michael gave him a nod that spoke of talk between men. "Sure. But if your dad was all right with it..." He left the option open.

"Maybe." Bobby shrugged, but his wistfulness was almost painful.

"Is Jim inside?" Suzanne asked.

Bobby looked up at them with eyes that were too old. He nodded, his voice dropping low. "He's not feeling so good today."

She brushed one hand over his hair, wishing she could do more. One step at a time, she reminded herself. Jim had insisted on being honest with Bobby, despite his age. Bobby knew Jim was dying, but she could see the hope for rescue in his eyes. It was a lot for a boy to handle, and they would all have to feel their way through this. "Is he up for visitors?"

Bobby looked up at her, leaning against her slightly. "He's pretty tired, but he wants to see you."

She wanted to snatch the boy up and hold him close, wanted to weep from the longing the slight pressure induced, to find some way to shield him from the pain to come. But some pain you just had to walk through. Vowing she would be there with him every step of the way, she forced herself to put a smile in her voice as she squeezed his thin shoulders. "I'd like to see him, too."

The three of them walked up the porch stairs and

headed inside, Maverick trailing them with the care-free abandon of someone who has known no heart-ache. Suzanne worried over how Jim might have de-teriorated, but he looked the same as ever, if a bit more pale.

He stood to greet them, but soon had to take his seat. Michael handled everything with a grace she was having difficulty summoning. He led them all into conversation about all manner of topics unrelated to illness and death and the life changes that were very near. Soon he had them all laughing, and Suzanne relaxed as she saw Bobby responding like a flower in the rain, drinking thirsty gulps of Michael's vibrancy, his good health and cheerful demeanor. She would have to trust Michael to keep the necessary distance, but at the moment, he was exactly what Bobby needed. His strength was giving Bobby back his childhood, even as she watched.

Soon Bobby had invited Michael to go outside and see a new trick he'd taught Maverick. Suzanne stayed inside at Jim's request.

"He's a good man," Jim observed. He was never one for a lot of words.

"He is."

"Think this might be more than temporary?"

She shook her head. "It's not what he wants. Not what we agreed." She leaned forward. "He'll be good to Bobby, Jim. He'll help me get him through the tough part. And even though we won't stay mar-

ried, we'll make it easy on Bobby. We'll stay friends,
I promise. Michael's even said he'd set up a college
fund.''

Jim frowned. ''Why would he do that?'' He shook
his head. ''Must have more money than I thought.''

''He does. I told him no, but I just wanted you to
know that's the kind of man he is. Decent. Really
decent.''

Jim studied her carefully. ''You might be wrong
about this lasting.''

She shook her head. She couldn't afford to hope.
''He's got his reasons. But we'll both work hard to
do right by Bobby.''

''Better work fast.''

She frowned. ''Why?''

''Things are getting worse real quick. Wish they
weren't.'' Naked pain washed over his face. ''I don't
want to leave him. He's all the son a man could ever
want.'' His voice cracked slightly, the most emotion
she'd ever heard from this very reserved man. He let
out a resigned sigh. ''But the good Lord has other
plans for me.''

His eyes pinned her. ''It's going a lot faster than
anyone thought, Suzanne. I can't keep things together
much longer. I need you to be ready to take him real
soon.''

''Oh, Jim.'' She reached for his hand.

''Don't feel sorry for me, hon. I'm not ready to
leave that boy, but I won't be sorry to get past this.

Days are gettin' hard now. Nights worse." He stared off into the distance for a moment, then squeezed her hand and pulled his back, straightening his shoulders with effort. "If you could see your way clear to picking him up Saturday and letting him spend the long weekend with you, I'd be obliged. And you might want to see about getting his school set up right away."

Oh, God. For a moment, panic flooded her. She wasn't ready. She'd wanted to take slow, careful steps so that Bobby could make the transition at his own pace and be completely comfortable by the time—

But Jim was telling her that time was a luxury he didn't have. Looking at him, she saw the exhaustion of constant pain and wondered how long he'd felt far worse than anyone knew.

Panic couldn't be allowed. She settled herself into her best social worker voice. "Michael's parents are throwing this party Friday night to celebrate the marriage, but we'll be here bright and early on Saturday, if that suits you."

He nodded, gratitude shining from weary eyes. "That would suit me just fine. Now if you'll help me up, we'll go outside and tell Bobby he's going to get to ride that horse sooner than he thought."

At his side, she headed for the door, promising herself that she would never let Bobby forget this brave and caring man who had been the best gift she could have ever given the child she'd had to let go. Now she would have him back, but she would make sure that Jim Roper lived on in her child's memory.

On Friday at six o'clock, Suzanne raced into the front door of Michael's house, knowing she'd barely have time for a shower and still not sure what she'd wear to the party. She'd decided days ago that the deep purple wool was the only thing she had that was remotely suitable, but she couldn't quit worrying that she'd embarrass Michael.

"Michael?" she called out. No answer. He was probably upstairs dressing. No time to waste. She all but ran up the stairs to her room.

When she opened the door, once again it slid over her—the sense of peace this room gave her. Never mind the awkwardness of having to knock to enter the dressing room they shared; never mind that in her mind the house was still Michael's and not hers.

This beautiful room, far lovelier than anything she'd ever dreamed of having, already felt like hers. Being here was almost like living in a luxury hotel.

She heard movement in the dressing room and couldn't help the quick skip of her heartbeat as the image of Michael half-clothed burned into her brain. She'd felt the power of his muscular frame, but in her private thoughts she had to admit that she'd like to see those muscles in the flesh. Did he have hair on his chest? What would his skin feel like against her

own? Would it be as heavenly as she'd imagined to
have him inside—

Stop. Don't go there, Suzanne. That way lies mad-
ness.

She shook her head and moved from where she'd
leaned against the door toward the delicate writing
desk in the corner to drop her briefcase. Okay, so she
lusted after Michael Longstreet. It didn't matter—
couldn't matter. He was her husband in name only.
They'd made rules.

But never, in a life full of rebellion, had she wanted
to break a rule more. Just once. Just one more taste
of being held in his arms.

No, no, no. Because if she knew one thing about
herself, it was that she'd never been good at keeping
her heart separate from her body. How she wished
she were a woman adept at using sex for sport, but
she wasn't. In the ten years since Bobby's father,
she'd been involved with exactly two men—and both
times, she'd led with her heart and wound up with it
broken. They'd wanted a strictly physical relationship; she'd wanted more.

Michael had made himself very clear that he was
open to a physical relationship but that his heart was
not available. Even if Bobby weren't in the picture,
that should be warning enough. Don't go there.

She set down her briefcase and purse and listened
for sounds of activity in the dressing room. Thus far,
they'd avoided the need for locks on either door, but

sometimes at night when she heard him moving around in there, she'd wished he weren't so honorable. She'd never breach the barrier, but if he did...

Suzanne shook her head hard and turned around, mentally cataloging what she needed to take with her to the bathroom across the hall.

And then she noticed the dress bag hanging on the door of the antique wardrobe across the room, marked with the name of a very exclusive dress shop in San Francisco.

For a moment she closed her eyes, not sure whether to smile or scream. Very slowly she walked toward it and lowered the zipper.

Suzanne caught her lower lip in her teeth. It was the most beautiful dress she'd ever seen, a silk confection spun of moonlight and amethysts. She pushed aside the dress bag and let her gaze feast on it, forbidden longing oozing from her every pore.

It was a long column of iridescent lavender and silver that would do amazing things to her eyes. Strapless and simple in line, the top beaded with a delicate fringe of silver bugle beads and amethyst crystals, it would nip in slightly at her waist and fall to her ankles in one shimmering column. On the floor stood a shoe box she was almost afraid to open—but of course, she did. Inside were silver evening sandals that were a perfect match.

She'd never seen anything so beautiful in her life, and she was torn between shame and gratitude. Michael knew her limited income and might have simply worried about her embarrassing him and his parents, no matter what he'd said. But that he would even think to do this for her...

Her eyes narrowed. Maybe he hadn't done this for her. Maybe he'd only done it for himself.

She whirled and stalked to the dressing room door, rapping sharply on it. When there was no answer, she barged inside, fist poised to rap on his bedroom door.

But it opened before she could touch it, and Suzanne fell speechless.

First at Michael in a tux. God, he was gorgeous, and it made her temper spike. He'd known this was formal and he hadn't told her.

"You big jerk," she sputtered. "You knew and you didn't tell me. When was I supposed to find out that this was formal? When I showed up in—"

"You're welcome." The green eyes that had at first been warm were cooling rapidly, as was his voice. "I'm so glad you like the dress. Please don't bother saying thank you," he responded dryly.

Shame sent her temper spiking. "I didn't ask you to buy me a dress. I'm not going to wear—"

"Fine." His tone was weary. "Wear whatever you want. But if you don't mind, we need to leave in half an hour. If you don't like it, I'll send it back."

"I can't afford that dress, Michael. And you should have told me. I could have made a horrible mistake. Your parents—" She was shocked to hear her voice break, to feel the press of tears, humiliated tears. She hadn't cried as much in the last ten years as she had in the last week.

"Suzanne, I wasn't trying to embarrass you. I wanted you to feel comfortable, and I knew that no matter how hard I tried to get my parents to make it simple and casual, my mother would insist on making too much of this. If I'd asked you first, you would have told me no, right?"

He nodded, though she hadn't answered. "Of course you would have." He shrugged his very broad shoulders, and despite her furious embarrassment, she couldn't help but admire the figure he cut in a tux that was obviously tailored just for him. "I didn't want to make you dread it all week, so I took matters into my own hands. If you hate the dress, don't wear it."

She glanced past him. "I don't hate it. It's the most beautiful thing I've ever—" Suddenly it registered on her what lay behind him. "That's your room?"

Michael shifted in the doorway and gestured for her to enter. She was already inside before the doubts hit her and she stopped in her tracks.

The room was stunning, thoroughly masculine, yet a room in which a woman could feel at home with a few softening touches. Mostly what she felt was a sense of welcome, a sense of refuge from the world outside. A huge four-poster bed topped by a deep forest-green comforter dominated the room, and it

looked out over the mountains, opening onto a panorama that was absolutely stunning. She could just
imagine sitting in that bed, propped up on pillows and
drinking coffee in the mornings. What a way to start
the day.

"Wow." She turned to Michael. "What a great
room." But she was already turning back to study
what had caught her gaze off to one side. "I figured
you must have your own bath, since there was nothing
of yours in the hall bath, not even a razor."

"I told you the other day that you could look
around."

"I didn't want to invade your privacy." But she
couldn't help cocking her head to one side, wishing
she could see further to figure out why there was so
much light coming from the bathroom.

He touched the small of her back slightly. "Go
ahead and look." He cast a quick look at his watch,
and she remembered the time.

"Never mind." But she was really curious.

One dimple winked at her, still such an odd sight
in such a rugged, very masculine face. "Go ahead.
You know you're dying to look. It's really pretty
great, if I do say so myself. It's one of the parts I
remodeled."

So she walked across the thick rug in greens and
golds and browns, thinking that Michael's room
brought the mountains inside, both with the huge windows and the colors he'd chosen.

At the door, she stopped in shock. "Wow" was all she could think to say.

Remnants of sunlight cascaded down from a skylight, as well as from the huge window over a whirlpool tub. No expense had been spared, from the steam bath shower to the expanses of marble to the tile floors. The mirrors over the vanity reflected the mountains and trees outside.

Suzanne smiled. "I could live in this room."

He met her smile. "I feel the same. It's self-indulgent, I know, but—" He shrugged. Then his eyes darkened. "If you wanted to borrow it sometimes—"

She shook her head rapidly, almost frantically. She saw him reflected in the mirrors, standing behind her, his powerful body sheltering hers, so male, so enticing. Visions of his hands on her, of being naked in that tub swamped her brain so fast she felt light-headed...visions of being skin to skin with Michael, of lying in that huge bed...of Michael naked in—

"No." Her voice was too sharp, she knew, but it was her only defense against a gut-deep longing that accompanied the visions.

Knowing she should apologize, she lifted her gaze to his, to see his eyes darkening with a preternatural awareness of her thoughts.

He wanted her, too. She could see it, could feel it in her bones. Longing shimmered up her spine, desire tugging low in her belly.

"Suzanne…" His voice was low and far too tempting. The man could tempt a saint. He took one step closer to her.

She stepped around him. "Michael, I can't." Poised to flee, she made herself turn and face him. "I'm sorry. It's not that I— It's just that—" How did she explain?

His eyes went soft and just a little sad. "You don't have to explain. I understand." His voice was gentle, if a little rough around the edges. "Why don't you go get dressed?"

She studied him for a long moment, wishing things were different. Wishing she were someone else, someone who would be a fitting match for this man, someone without a past. But she couldn't wish Bobby away, nor did she want to do so. Her choice was clear and could be her only focus. And Michael had made it very, very clear that he did not want another family.

"I'm sorry," she said again. And then she fled.

Michael watched her walk down the stairs, so solemn, so uncertain, and struggled to draw in a deep, calming breath. The scene in his bedroom and his far-too-strong wish to keep her there, to tumble her to his bed, had been unsettling enough. But this dress. Sweet mercy. He'd done too well. And it wasn't really the dress. It was the dress on her. She looked like a goddess wrapped in moonlight and dreams, her vivid coloring the perfect foil for the seductive mystery of the silk.

He hadn't intended it to be seductive—God knows, he didn't need her to be any more so than she already was—he'd merely chosen the dress for how it seemed to complement her beautiful eyes. Her very sad eyes, so full of confusion and worry and way too many nerves. Lightly, she touched the cameo at her throat as though it would protect her.

He realized he hadn't spoken yet, hadn't told her. Both of them could use some lightening up, so he let out a long, low wolf whistle.

When she grinned and color stained her cheeks, he knew he'd chosen right. Keep it light, Longstreet. She's nervous enough. Help her enjoy the night. "You look like a million bucks. I'll never get a chance to dance with you."

Fear stabbed the violet orbs. "You said you'd—"

He crossed to where she stood and looked down at her. With the heels, she was tall enough that he didn't have to bend down so much. "I promised you I'd stay with you as long as you needed me, and I meant it." Then he forced a grin when he found himself wanting to growl. "But I'm going to have to bloody some noses to keep the guys away."

Her smile was wide and genuine. "You think so?" She glanced down, then back up. "Michael, you shouldn't have, but it's the most beautiful dress I've ever seen. I don't know how much—"

He pressed one finger to her lips, then jerked it away as if burned. "If you say one more word about money tonight, I won't be responsible for my actions." He stroked her chin gently. "Please. Forget the cost of the dress. I can afford it. Just try to enjoy it instead of getting mad." He smiled. "Besides, I'm about to make you madder."

"What does that mean?"

"It's a surprise."

Her gaze narrowed.

"Close your eyes."

Slowly, suspicion in every line of her frame, still she did so.

He pulled a square box from his pocket, removing one earring from it. Mounted on amethysts lay cameos of palest alabaster to match the heirloom necklace. Gently, before she could react, he slid aside her hair and fastened the earring to one delicate lobe.

"Michael, what—"

He concentrated hard on fastening the second earring with his too-large fingers.

And tried not to think about the silken skin he couldn't help but brush.

"Michael, no, you can't—"

"There," he sighed. "Finally. I was afraid I'd hurt you." He drew her toward the mirror in the foyer and held her before him, his hands on her bare shoulders, reluctant to move them away no matter how her skin burned under his palms. "What do you think?"

She leaned back against him slightly, her eyes wide and round and confused. Too quickly she pulled herself away, and he had to fight himself not to draw her back against him, hard. The delicate spot where neck and shoulder joined was bared to him and he wanted badly to place his mouth there, to tempt her to surrender to him, to test the strength of the wanting he saw in her eyes, day after day.

Her breasts rose with her indrawn breath, and his gaze slid to the shadowed valley between the tender slopes. It would be so very, very easy to slide his hands down from her shoulders, to cup her breasts in his palms, to nudge aside the fabric, to turn her around and bend her over and put his mouth—

"They're beautiful."

He snapped out of fantasy and tried to concentrate on her words. "You like them?"

"How could I not? Look at them," she sighed.

"They almost do you justice," he said, unable to help sliding his hands down her arms. "They're almost worthy of your beauty."

She blushed again and shook her head, swaying back against him slightly. "You don't have to say I'm beautiful just to be nice, Michael."

The contact burned. He had to stop this now or they would never make it out of this house, his conscience be damned. He removed his hands from her and moved away quickly, flicking her a grin he hoped looked more casual than he felt. "Too bad you're not up for a quick fling, Suzanne. I'd show you just how little 'nice' plays a part in my behavior.''

She stiffened, and though it was what he'd intended—to gain distance by reminding her that any relationship could only be physical—he couldn't quite congratulate himself. But his need to have her was getting stronger by the day, and he could see no way for them to win.

She pulled the silk shawl that had come with the dress up around her shoulders and tilted her chin up in defiance. ''Did it ever occur to you that a quick fling might not be enough? That maybe even Love 'Em and Leave 'Em Longstreet might meet his match one day?''

Oh yeah. It certainly had. But no way was he telling her that, not with this ache for her eating a hole in his belly. They were moving closer every day to a conflagration he knew they must avoid. He couldn't fall in love, but she could—and he could definitely see the potential to want to keep her in his bed for a long, long time. Down that road lay a host of problems and, all wanting aside, he liked Suzanne too much to let that happen.

''I never said you didn't make me want to chew through walls to get to you, Suzanne.'' He escorted her toward the door. ''But I think we both know it would be a big mistake.''

She nodded up at him, her eyes huge and solemn. ''The biggest.''

He tried not to feel insulted as he led her outside. "You'll let me know, though, if your base desires overcome you, right? If you suddenly come to your senses and see the wisdom of using me for my body?" He grinned past a faint ache.

Suzanne laughed then, and if it was a little strained, it was still musical and welcome. "You'll be the first to know, Mr. Mayor. That I can promise."

But her tone made it very clear that he shouldn't be holding his breath.

As they approached the Longstreets' enormous mountain home, ablaze with lights and music, Suzanne's stomach clenched. Valet parking, sophisticated women, silver-haired men who moved with the grace of years of command and power...this was not a world she knew, not a world in which she fit.

Michael placed one large warm hand at the small of her back and leaned down. "Imagine them in their underwear. It'll do the trick every time."

She was too surprised to stem the laugh that bubbled up. Just that quickly, she relaxed and glanced up to catch his wink. "Stick with me, babe. Just remember, you can do no wrong. You're the golden girl who finally caught Romeo Rich Guy." He grinned as he threw her caustic phrase back at her and slid his arm around her waist, catching her against him for one too-brief hug.

Then they were inside, being greeted by a couple

who could have stepped out of the pages of *Vanity Fair.* "Hello, Suzanne," Grace Longstreet said. The tall woman, slim, elegant and champagne blond, leaned down to press her cheek to Suzanne's. "We're so very happy to meet you at last." She clasped Suzanne's hand between both of hers, and Suzanne was startled to see Mrs. Longstreet's eyes—Michael's eyes—brimming with unshed tears. "I hope you'll let me take you to lunch soon to chat, just us girls. I can't tell you what this marriage means to us."

Suzanne felt like a fraud; nonetheless she smiled and agreed, but then Michael led her gently to his father. Looking at John Longstreet showed Suzanne just how wonderfully Michael would age. She knew the older man was very frail but he still stood straight and tall, his thick shock of white hair so dignified that she almost missed the kind blue eyes that studied her thoughtfully.

He leaned down from a height almost as great as Michael's and grasped her hand, his voice a warm, soothing baritone. He looked at the Longstreet cameo at her throat, glanced at his son solemnly, then back at her. And smiled. "You've made an old man very happy, my dear. If this son of mine doesn't make you blissfully happy, you just tell me and I'll straighten him out." His smile flashed white and gleaming as he spoke a little softer. "But I'm almost certain my son is not foolish enough to let a gorgeous creature like you out of his grasp. Not when I see that you're

not only beautiful but intelligent and caring, as well.''
He patted one hand on top of their joined hands.
''Welcome to the family, Suzanne. You've given us
a dream.''

He was so warm and kind and genuine that she
could barely stand continuing the lie. She glanced
over at Michael to see a plea in his gaze. She thought
of how he'd extended himself for Bobby and knew
she could do no less, no matter what kind of fraud
that made her.

So she spoke from the heart, as far as circumstance
would permit. ''Your son is a wonderful man,'' she
said honestly. ''You've done well by him.'' Then, just
as Michael had accused her of doing, she acted on
impulse and wrapped her arms around John Longstreet's shoulders, giving him a quick hug.

He returned the hug, and she could feel the brittle-
ness of his bones beneath his perfectly fitted tux. A
faint tremble in his shoulders told her just how much
a strain this evening was putting on him. When they
moved apart, she thought she might be able to do
what no one else here could and get him to sit down,
so she whispered to him, ''My feet are killing me in
these high-heeled sandals. Would you be willing to
help me find someplace to sit down?''

He cast her a glance that said he knew exactly what
she was doing, then looked at his son and his wife.
''Excuse me, son. I'm going to go hold court with
the star of tonight's show.''

Michael shot her a warm glance filled with pride. "I'll help Mother with the receiving line while you two take a break."

She felt a light touch on her shoulder and turned to see Grace mouth a thank-you, her look one of immense gratitude, before she turned to the next guest.

And so it was that Suzanne passed a good hour sitting on a large sofa falling in love with Michael's father as he introduced friends and made her feel completely at home and at ease. She knew from the first moment she met his parents that she could give no less than her best, not simply for the sake of her bargain with Michael, but for the sake of these very kind and generous people.

Soon Grace Longstreet came over and visited with them a bit. Her questions were more incisive than her husband's, and Suzanne had to do some fancy footwork to keep their cover story intact. When Michael showed up to ask her to dance, she accepted with relief, bending first to kiss his father's cheek. "Thank you both for making me feel so welcome. I see now why Michael is such a good man."

They were still beaming at her when Michael whirled her away to the dance floor. "Thank you," he said. His eyes were a soft warm green now. "I haven't seen my dad that energized in a long, long time."

"He's a wonderful man, Michael. They're both so kind."

"My mother's very impressed, and she doesn't impress easily."

"You said she was desperate. She's probably just grateful I have all my teeth."

He laughed. "You're right, they weren't going to be picky, but you come as a huge relief. My mother, who isn't exactly a libertine, even said she could see why you could provoke me to something so impulsive."

"What does that mean?"

"It's my mother's very polite way of saying you're a knockout."

Suzanne rolled her eyes.

Michael whirled her around, and Suzanne's head felt light. "It's true," he said.

The admiration in his eyes was heady and sent her spirits soaring. She felt like nothing so much as Cinderella at the ball with the prince, while the king and queen watched and smiled fondly. She was somewhere outside herself, not Suzanne Jorgenson anymore but some fairy creature who could be Suzanne Longstreet, a woman who would wear beautiful dresses, who would belong in a place like this. She floated on the music, the glitter of the sparkling chandelier, the enchantment of this magical evening.

Michael pulled her close, and her breasts rubbed his chest, her thighs brushed his own. She could feel him harden against her. He leaned in and brushed her ear with his lips. "I want you, Suzanne."

Warm breath whispered down her neck, and Suzanne shivered. "Michael, we agreed—"

"I know what we agreed. I didn't say this was smart." But his large warm hand slid up her back and caressed naked skin. For a moment, he held her so close she could barely breathe from the overload to her every nerve. He was so big, so larger than life in many ways, that he swamped her senses, made it hard to remember anything when he was in the room. Feeling him against her, feeling his body's response stirred something deep inside her.

She tightened her fingers on the back of his neck, sliding them upward into his hair while she pressed her face into his shoulder and tried to remember why she shouldn't crave his touch. She opened her eyes and realized they were in a dark alcove. She started to speak, but suddenly his mouth was on hers, hot and dark and demanding.

With a whimper, she gave in, answering his kiss with all the hunger that had been building for days. Michael took her mouth and gave no quarter, the easygoing man nowhere in sight. The man who held her now kissed her with power and barely leashed passion, his tongue sweeping inside and taking control. His kiss was alternately rough and sweet, fiery and tempting as his strong arms surrounded her, making her feel both protected and all but ravaged.

He broke away for one second, his eyes more vulnerable than she'd ever seen them. "Kiss me," he said roughly. "Kiss me back."

It was what she wanted, what she'd wanted since that first night. Past her defenses he stole like a thief in the darkness. She fell headlong into temptation, pressing her body against his, heedless of anything but this man, this night. When she heard Michael groan and felt his hands on her body, she wanted to strip them both naked, wanted to surrender to his magnetism, to the full power of her own passion, her own greed. Her head spun with magic and delicious fear, climbing toward a high, exhilarating peak, teetering on the edge of some sweet, terrifying ecstasy she'd never known, but wanted desperately. She wasn't afraid; she wanted only to go closer and closer to danger until she stood on the edge of that cliff and felt the wind whip her hair and sting her face.

They could have magic between them, if only Michael would believe in love and open his heart. "Oh, Michael, could we make this work?" She let longing and hope spill into every word.

Suddenly he stiffened and stopped, his hands falling to his side. With eyes gone dark with fathoms-deep pain, he looked at her as if he'd never seen her before. "Suzanne, I can't—" He stepped back, his hands out as if to ward her off. "I'm not— God, I can't do this. I love Elaine, I can't—" He stared off into the distance behind her, and she could see him closing the doors and locking them tight, every bit of vulnerability gone as though it never existed.

A muscle leaped in his jaw. Finally he spoke, still not looking at her. "That was inexcusable, so I won't even ask you to try." He glanced down, and once again the stranger with the cold malachite eyes looked at her. But even as he looked at her, they wavered once. But only once.

She wanted to argue with him, to scream that Elaine was dead and she was alive and she could love him if he'd just let her in.

But they had a bargain. And she had her pride. She'd begged one man to love her and he'd tried to buy his way out. She would not beg Michael for something he was unwilling to give.

"I'd like to leave now," she said, keeping her gaze carefully focused on the drapes behind him. If she looked at him, she had the sinking feeling that she would cry.

"Wait here and I'll tell my parents that you're exhausted. There's a way out the back."

"No." Though she wanted desperately to steal away and hide, she would show him she was made of sterner stuff. It wasn't his parents' fault that her heart had so unwisely overstepped the boundaries already set. She wouldn't shame them. She tilted her chin and spoke. "I'm going to say a proper goodbye."

She thought she saw respect glimmer in his gaze

as he nodded. "Fine." He reached out to take her elbow, and it was all she could do not to shrug him off. But they were playing a game, and Suzanne Jorgenson never, ever quit before the end.

# Nine

If only Bobby would cry, Suzanne thought. His anguish was palpable, his desire to return home to Jim so obvious and strong that it tore her heart out. But he sat in the back seat of Michael's Explorer with one arm around Maverick, his dear little face very pale, his blue eyes huge, his body still. Too still for a young boy, as though it took everything he had.

Bless Michael. Before they picked Bobby up, the atmosphere in the car had been beyond strained. After last night, after that strange, sudden chill when seconds before she and Michael had both been red-hot, he'd taken her home without another word between them. She'd heard him pace in his room, then go back down the stairs as she lay sleepless at 3:00 a.m. This morning they'd passed like ships in the night, stepping around each other for coffee, neither one interested in food.

But he hadn't taken it out on her son. He'd been the soul of kindness to a very lost little boy. When they arrived, she discovered that he'd arranged for a nurse to come stay with Jim so Bobby would have no reason to worry about his dad being alone. He'd offered Bobby conversation once they got on the road, but he hadn't pushed nor shown discomfort when Bobby spoke little. He'd made it all seem natural and comfortable.

Suzanne wished she could do the same, but she was so afraid of saying the wrong thing, of making all this harder on Bobby. And she still didn't know how or when to let Bobby know she was his mother, though her heart cried out to tell him that he was home again, where he belonged.

She couldn't do that, because it wasn't home to him. Home meant Jim Roper to her son.

When they turned on the road leading up to Michael's place, she heard Maverick begin to whine.

"Think he needs out, Bobby?" Michael asked.

"Yes, sir. He probably does."

"Can he wait another two minutes, you think, or should we let him out now?"

Suzanne wished she could tell Michael how much

it meant that he treated Bobby with such respect instead of talking down to him as so many did.

He would be such a wonderful father, if only he'd open his heart.

"I think he'll make it, sir, but I don't know if you want to risk it."

Michael looked into the rearview mirror. "You think he'll make it, I'm betting on you."

She saw the flush of pride on that very young face. Then suddenly Bobby's gaze lit, and for the first time that day, he wore a smile.

"Are those your horses?"

"Sure are. See that paint over on the right?"

"Yes, sir."

"That's Daisy. That's the one I'm thinking might fit just right for you."

"She's big." Faint nerves whispered in his voice.

"She is, but she's a sweetheart. Not too easy," Michael pointed out, saving Bobby's pride. "She'll take some handling. Think you're up to it?"

Bobby was straining at his seat belt. "I don't know, but I sure want to try."

Michael chuckled. "That's the spirit." He stopped the Explorer. "We can see the house later, if you want. Let's let Maverick out, but keep him on his leash so he doesn't get kicked. He's not used to horses, is he?"

"No, sir."

"Well, we'll train him, but I'd hate for him to have to learn the hard way."

Boy and dog tumbled out, Maverick barking for joy and straining at the leash in his eagerness to confront the huge threats to his beloved master. Bobby dropped down on his knees and talked earnestly to the dog. Maverick dropped his bottom to the ground, tail wagging fiercely.

"Why don't I take Maverick so Michael can show you the horses?" Suzanne suggested.

Gratitude shone from her son's gaze. "You wouldn't mind?"

"Not a bit," she replied, eager to do anything that would keep a smile on his face. "I like dogs." She leaned down and ruffled the black fur. "Especially this one." Maverick rewarded her with a big slurp on the cheek.

Bobby laughed, and it was music to her ears.

She wanted to be everything Bobby ever needed, but it was Michael who had the magic elixir now to banish Bobby's heartache, so she would wait.

Her patience was rewarded when Michael put Bobby up on Daisy's bare back and kept the mare still while her son petted her. When Bobby leaned down impulsively and hugged the huge neck, Suzanne smiled through tears of gratitude.

But when he turned that same beaming gaze onto Michael, hero worship already evident, Suzanne's heart seized.

She couldn't blame Bobby. There was much to love about Michael Longstreet.

But Michael Longstreet didn't want to be loved.

With quick steps, she headed for the pen to break up a bond that would only bring her child heartache.

Michael entered his office on Tuesday after a long holiday weekend that had been interrupted several times by concerned citizens wanting to know if the FBI or EPA had yet determined how the water at Hopechest had become contaminated. He'd spent hours both in person and on the phone, reassuring the citizens that everything possible had been done. He'd even taken Suzanne and Bobby to town twice to make it conspicuous that he would remain in Prosperino for the duration, along with those he loved.

No one had blinked at seeing Suzanne with yet another charge in her custody. She'd always taken the Hopechest kids around town with her, trying to weave them into the community. Everyone seemed inclined to believe that Bobby was such a child.

It had to be Suzanne's call as to when she revealed that he was her child. Michael thought she was foolish to wait, but Bobby was not his concern. Couldn't be, no matter how engaging the boy was or how much Michael wished he could shield Bobby from the pain of losing his dad.

Too often, Michael had caught himself comparing Bobby to the age his own son would be. John Michael would be eight now, and Bobby's presence, his vigor, his sheer joy in living rebuked Michael every day, every hour.

Sometimes, just for a second, Michael allowed himself to think that it was his son there before him, the blue eyes instead Elaine's brown, the frame tall and bony as Michael had been in boyhood. More than once, he'd caught his hand hovering over Bobby's head, wanting to touch the hair, wanting to hug the thin shoulders, to close his eyes and imagine....

He didn't honestly know how he was going to handle having Bobby live with them full-time. He didn't question his ability to be good to the boy. Bobby was a great kid anyone could enjoy—bright, kindhearted, braver than anyone had the right to expect of someone so young.

But he wasn't Michael's son, wasn't the child Michael had wanted so badly to raise to manhood, and every hour spent with Suzanne's child made him ache for what was lost. Made him want things he could not allow himself to need.

He already wanted Suzanne far too much. He could not want her child, too. He'd gone too far, too fast, too deep that night at the party. The power of the response Suzanne drew from him mocked his love for Elaine, the woman with whom his heart had died long ago. He had made a vow over a grave that should never have been. It was fitting penance for his pride.

He could desire Suzanne, but he could give her no more. When he'd seen more in her eyes, seen hope spark, and felt her melt against him, he'd tried to resist, knowing she deserved better than what he could give her.

But something about her had called to him, had slid down deep inside him, far past the place he'd declared forbidden to anyone but the wife and child he'd lost.

It had been a long time since Michael had felt fear, but fear held him fast in its grip now. Suzanne was dangerous far beyond her physical appeal, mighty as it was. Something about her beckoned and made him want more than he could have.

They'd made a bargain, and she'd made the ground rules clear. Yes, she'd responded to him with an intensity that even now made him hunger. But she didn't want to want him, nor did he want to crave her. They were oil and water, and there was an innocent boy to consider.

A boy who touched something too deep inside him.

A boy she would take away from him one day very soon.

When the phone rang, Michael welcomed the interruption to the tangle that had become his life. When he heard what the FBI agent had to say, all thought of Suzanne and Bobby slipped into the background.

*   *   *

Suzanne drove from the Coltons' to Michael's office, every nerve inside her shivering with both anticipation and dread.

It was happening too fast, and she could no longer kid herself that she could manage everything without a hitch. The call from Cousin Edna had thrown her into turmoil.

Jim had been taken to the hospital after collapsing, his condition worsening rapidly. Bobby was still at school, unaware that anything had changed. Cousin Edna had been notified first and wanted to know how Suzanne proposed to handle things now. Edna's conviction that it would devastate Bobby to have to change schools now had been communicated clearly. She wanted to keep him there in the same town and the same school, all but accusing Suzanne of selfishness in taking Bobby away.

It was Suzanne's first encounter with Edna, and the woman had made it very clear that Suzanne was suspect, that she had to prove herself. Suzanne longed to be able to respond definitively, but she wasn't a free agent. Any decision she made impacted Michael. Not for the first time, she rued the day they'd concocted this scheme. Left on her own, she had autonomy to do whatever was needed for her son. But left on her own, her chances for custody dimmed considerably.

And she was not on her own, no matter how distant Michael had been with her since the scorching kisses at the party she wished she'd never attended.

Parking the car, she practically ran into Michael's office, racing past his secretary. When she pushed open the partially closed door, she saw him staring out the window, his hands in his pockets, his broad shoulders slightly bent.

But as she entered, he whirled, the deep worry on his face making way for a puzzled frown. "What's wrong?"

"It's Jim—he's collapsed. He's in the hospital. Bobby doesn't know, but it doesn't look good and Edna—" She swallowed hard. "Edna wants to know why I think it's right to take Bobby out of school there when everything else in his life is out of control. She wants to keep him there until Jim—" She swallowed hard against the lump in her throat. She had to think. She couldn't cry. Bowing her head, she fought back treacherous tears.

She heard his steps across the carpet. Strong arms came around her, pulling her close. Despite what she knew was smart, Suzanne let her head rest, just for a moment, against Michael's broad chest. Let his big warm hand sweep up and down her back while she listened to the comforting beat of his heart. How she wished she could stay right here.

But she could not. She had to be strong for her son. No matter how wonderful his arms felt, Michael would not be part of their lives for long and she couldn't afford to get used to the comfort. She straightened and pulled back from the tempting refuge.

He let her go and stepped away, shoving his hands back into his pockets. "So what do you want to do?"

"I don't know what's right. I want him with me so I can protect him, so I can help him deal with—" She thought of Jim, so kind and caring, lying near death. She wanted her son, but not at the cost of that good man's life. She lifted her gaze. "Am I being selfish, Michael? Am I doing the wrong thing, wanting custody of him?"

His eyes held only sympathy as he lifted a hand to her hair. "He's your son. Of course you want him. And Jim believes Bobby belongs with you."

"But what about Edna? Maybe I should leave Bobby with her until—"

Michael shook his head. "There's no way to make this clean and easy for him, Suzanne. Life isn't like that. Bobby is stronger than you realize. He's had to accept a lot already, and what's most important is that he knows he's not alone, that he knows that no matter how much he misses his dad, he has shelter and refuge he can count on. That there is love ready to fill in the emptiness whenever he's ready to accept it."

Suzanne looked at Michael and wished he could apply those same words to himself, but there was as much chance of that as of her sprouting wings. So she shut her mind to an avenue that would lead nowhere and turned her concentration to the pressing needs of her son. "So you think I should go get him?"

"He's your son, Suzanne. Only you can decide."

"But—" She stifled the words. He was right, except for one thing. "This impacts you, too. Are you ready to have him with us full-time?"

Naked pain crossed his face, and she knew he was thinking about the child he'd lost. Several times over the weekend she'd caught him staring at Bobby with the same expression, mingled with a longing that tore at her heart.

"It doesn't matter if I am or not. The time has come, and I'll do what's needed."

She knew he would. He'd made that abundantly clear by his actions over the weekend. A few times he'd disappeared outside and been gone for hours, but when he was with Bobby, she couldn't fault his treatment of her son. He was kind if distant, and Bobby had soaked up his strong male presence like a plant after a long drought.

"I have to go to Bobby. Can you come with me?"

Michael shook his head. "Sorry, not right now." He glanced at the phone. "That was the FBI. They've figured out the source of the contamination. The DMBE came from Springer, and it appears it was intentional."

She blinked. "The Springer refinery here, outside town? Someone did it on purpose? Why would— Who would poison a bunch of kids?"

His expression was grim. "That's not the worst part of it. There are still barrels missing, and there's no way to know if all the chemicals have been used or someone's waiting to dump more. Prosperino could still be in danger. All hell's going to break loose when word gets around.''

Her eyes flew wide open. "Oh, my God."

"Maybe you should stay at Jim's house with Bobby until I know more."

"Come with me, Michael."

"You know I can't. I have to stay here. People will panic. They'll want to evacuate, and I can't blame them, but someone's got to stay here. There could be looting of the empty houses, and Prosperino's not exactly flush with extra cops."

"What about National Guard troops?"

He frowned. "That would only incite more panic. Right now the water's testing all right and plenty of water's being trucked in, but we're planning for emergency evacuation if the DMBE starts to show up. That hasn't changed, but we can't breathe easy until those missing barrels are found—and until the FBI figures out who's responsible. I don't want you and Bobby in the middle of this."

"Michael, I can't go off and leave you—" She broke off as quick awareness flared in his gaze. Leaving him was exactly what she intended to do one day soon.

"Go see Jim and take care of your son, Suzanne. Don't let Edna get her hooks into the situation. I'll call you later, once I get past the press conference that starts in an hour. If I can get away, I'll come over tonight, but if not, I'll be in touch.'' He wrote a number on a piece of paper, then handed it to her. "Take my cell phone number, in case you need me.''

She studied him carefully, seeing the lines of strain on his face. A lot of people looked to him to keep things calm and settled, and he couldn't even find peace in his own home, thanks to her. She needed to go to Bobby, but she had to say this first. Drawing a deep breath, she looked him straight in the eyes. "Michael, I didn't know how hard this would be for you, or I would never have agreed. I can take my chances with Edna if you'd rather we stopped this charade right now.''

His eyes studied her solemnly. "I'm not letting you down. I gave my word.''

"I can't tell how difficult it's going to get. You didn't bargain on all of this. I was naive when I thought this could be done.''

He shook his head, his jaw resolute. "We said we'd do our best to honor the vows we took while we were together. I think 'for better or for worse' was included.''

He was such a decent man. A man a woman could love so very easily. Her heart cried out for his.

But his heart was not available. Only his protection was.

And she didn't have the luxury of turning it down. Edna's voice had been full of menace, full of certainty that Suzanne would come up short. Maybe she was far from certain herself that she would be the perfect mother, but all Suzanne had to do was remember the light in Bobby's eyes when he was at Michael's place, to hear the hard, cold tone of Cousin Edna, to know that Bobby's spirit would die with that woman, no matter how well Edna cared for his physical well-being.

Maybe Suzanne wasn't the perfect mother yet, but she loved Bobby, body and soul. She'd told a hundred parents that the root of a child's well-being lay in love, fierce, consuming love. She had that and more.

She reached out to Michael and laid her hand on his chest, over his heart. With everything that was in her, she spoke. "You are a very good man, Michael. The best. I pray to the heavens that I'm not doing you harm when I say thank you from the bottom of my heart. For my son and for myself, I want you to know that I'm very, very sorry for anything we do that hurts you. I'm going to be selfish for Bobby's sake and keep this charade going, but I want you to have my pledge that I will end it as soon as humanly possible. And I will be forever in your debt."

Pain washed over his face, and she'd never seen him more solemn than when he placed his large hand over hers. "I don't want you in my debt, Suzanne. You owe me nothing. If I can help you keep your child, maybe it will make up, in some small measure, for what I cost Elaine."

She could feel the grief inside him, the dark sorrow that festered there. She wished for the power to reach down into his heart and heal the wounds that haunted him still.

But he would not let her—he'd made that clear. His pain was his own, and jealously guarded. He paid homage to a dead woman, and Suzanne could not break that bond, no matter how she wished it. She wanted to believe that given enough time together, free of distractions, she could change that.

But they did not have time, nor freedom. Prosperino needed Michael, and Bobby needed her. So they would part.

She rose to her toes and kissed his cheek, fighting back the deep ache of sorrow. "You deserve better, Michael Longstreet. I wish I could make you see that."

Then, before she broke down, she turned and left, clutching the scrap of paper in her hand.

# Ten

As he walked downstairs, yawning, Michael couldn't remember the last time he slept for more than two hours. Suzanne had been staying with Bobby for a week now, and it seemed like a year. The house felt twice as empty as it had before she'd moved in.

And it would be emptier still when she left. Her laughter, her ability to find joy so easily—they would be gone. He would miss her bright mind, her fiery spirit more than he could have ever imagined. They were opposites in so many ways, but she charged the atmosphere simply by being around.

He glanced at the profusion of plants in the break-fast area, frowning as he noticed that a couple were drooping. As much as Suzanne cherished them, he'd better not let them die. Rubbing one hand over the top of his head, he yawned again. First he'd start the coffee, then he'd water the plants.

A little while later, plants watered and a full mug in hand, he stared out at the mountain vista he'd loved so much, but he saw no trees or slopes. Instead, he thought about Suzanne. And Bobby. He wondered how Jim Roper had passed the night.

And he remembered a terror of years long ago, of whispered conversations his mother had on the phone while trying to maintain the pose that everything was fine, that the father who was in a hospital he couldn't visit would come home one day soon and be just the way Michael remembered him.

Deep inside him, Michael could still recall how it felt to try to play along with his mother while terror gnawed at his insides. She couldn't hide her fear, and Michael had wished she would tell him the truth almost as much as he'd prayed she would not. It was clear to him, even at twelve, that he might never see his father again. In the middle of the night, he would kneel beside his bed and pray to a somewhat hazy concept of God to bring his father back, to make his mother smile again.

The small boy inside Michael reached out to the boy who was Suzanne's child, wishing he could turn away the far more terrible knowledge Bobby possessed. The boy was brave and stalwart. He was a boy any man would be proud to call son.

No. Even thinking that was a betrayal of the tiny baby boy who had never drawn one breath of air, who had never had a chance because Michael Longstreet had failed him. Michael's actions had led to the death of the only son he would ever have. To the death of the only woman he would ever love. She'd told him the brakes concerned her, but he hadn't checked them that day, too harried by school and his job, trying to show his parents that he could be a success without them. He'd refused to reconcile with them out of pride, and Elaine had suffered poverty along with him, when he could have made her life so easy, so fine.

They'd had an argument just before she left that day because he'd caught her placing a call to his parents and he could never take the harsh words back. Mother and child had perished together in the crash, and he'd sworn a vow over her grave that he would never replace her or their child, that he would spend his life making it count. The only alternative had been to end it, to let the endless, gnawing grief eat away at him until he took the ultimate step.

But that would have dishonored two lives that Michael had loved, if imperfectly. If with monumental failure.

If he could have loved a woman again, Suzanne would have been the one. If he could have taken a boy to his heart, Bobby would be that boy. But he'd promised Elaine and their child, lying together for eternity, that he would love no one else. He'd failed them in the worst possible way in life; he could not fail them in death.

And knowing that, the only thing left to do was to hold himself apart from Bobby and Suzanne and make it as easy for them to leave as possible, even if he spent the rest of his life feeling the emptiness that lay around him now.

The phone rang, and Michael picked it up. "Hello?"

"Michael?"

He could hear the tears in her voice. "What's wrong, Suzanne?"

"It's Jim. He's…gone, Michael. And Bobby—" Her voice broke. "He's—"

"I'll be there in an hour." He was already mentally composing a list of calls he had to make. "Hold on, Suzanne. I'll be with you soon."

"Thank you," she whispered. "You don't have to, but—" Tears crowded her voice.

"Just hold on, sweetheart. I won't be long."

"Thank you, Michael." She paused as if she wanted to say more.

And God help him, he wanted to hear it.

But he'd made a promise to a woman and a boy who could not release him.

* * *

It had been a very long week, and Suzanne was so
tired her bones ached. She'd been strong for Bobby.
She'd been strong for Jim. She'd even weathered
Cousin Edna's disapproval and attempts to take
Bobby home with her. Thank goodness Jim had been
lucid enough for brief moments to change his will.
Still, Edna watched her like a hawk.

It hadn't been until she'd heard Michael's voice on
the phone that the temptation to break down had almost overwhelmed her. He'd sounded so strong and
sure and had so quickly taken decisive steps that for
a moment, her strength had wavered under the on-
slaught of her need to let him take over.

But she couldn't do that. That luxury was not hers.
Bobby was her child, and he was reeling from the
blow that all his hopes, all his prayers had not kept
him from losing his father. So he could be her only
concern.

At almost ten, he was too big for her lap, but she
snuggled him close on the sofa, the cool wind wash-
ing over them through the open screen door, and he
didn't seek to leave her side. If anything, he leaned
into her more as he read to her from the book she'd
selected as a diversion.

Suddenly he stopped. "Michael's coming soon?"
In his blue eyes, so fragile with grief, she saw hope
shining.

That hope would have to die one day, but not this
day. It was not yet time to leave Michael. "Yes."

She nodded. "He said he'd be here in an hour and it's almost been that long."

"But he can't stay? Because he's the mayor?"

She'd tried to explain that a lot of other people needed him and that was why he couldn't come before, even though he called every day to talk to them both. "That's right, sweetie. Michael's taking care of the water problems, but some people don't understand the situation and they're scared, so Michael has to keep them calm."

"Hmmph—" Edna Waters walked into the room, drying her hands on a dish towel. "One more reason for Bobby to stay with us. Bad water. People will get sick."

Suzanne felt Bobby stiffen beside her. She knew he didn't want to go with Edna. He'd told her so more than once. "The situation is under control. No one's gotten sick yet. And no one will. Michael's had water trucked in ever since this started."

"If he were any kind of mayor, he'd evacuate the town instead of playing God with people's lives."

Bobby spoke up. "Michael's not like that. He cares about people and animals. He won't let anyone get—"

A deep voice intervened from the porch. "I'm certainly trying to keep that from happening."

"Michael!" Bobby was off the sofa in a shot, charging through the open door and into Michael's arms.

Suzanne watched as the big man wrapped his arms around her son and held him close. She saw Michael's eyes close over a dark, aching sorrow, and she heard Bobby's sobs begin, the sobs he hadn't let anyone else hear.

Michael opened his eyes for a moment and looked at her. He nodded his head toward the porch swing, waiting for approval.

She nodded, and Michael strode out of sight carrying her son, but she could hear his deep voice speaking in a calm, soothing tone.

She was happy for Bobby; she would have liked to be tucked against Michael herself.

"He hardly knows that man," Edna said. "But I'm glad the boy has him. He'll need someone to give him the guidance Jim can't."

Suzanne was surprised by the conciliatory tone. "Michael's a good man." She couldn't let herself think about the price of walking away. Maybe, just maybe, this would bring them closer. Maybe Bobby could do what she couldn't and bring Michael out of his own grief.

Once again that tiny seed of hope stirred, never mind that it had been crushed to powder more than once.

Edna moved closer to the window. "Come here." Her voice was softer than Suzanne had ever heard it. "Look at this."

Suzanne moved to the side of this woman who

wielded too much power for her to ever rest easy. She looked out the window.

Bobby was cradled in Michael's lap, falling asleep as tears dried on his cheeks. Michael rocked him, slowly and softly, staring out into the distance, his face naked with pain.

Edna wiped her hands again, then pinned Suzanne with a stare. "That man's the best thing you got going for you. I see this, and I know Bobby's in good hands."

Suzanne's feathers ruffled. She was a good mother. Michael shouldn't matter.

But he did, and she would take any edge she could get. If Edna liked Michael's effect on Bobby, then Suzanne would remain quiet and work steadily to secure custody of her son before Edna could know that Michael never intended to be Bobby's true father.

"He is in good hands," Suzanne said, trying to stifle the shaft of fear that swept through her as she thought of how painful it would be to leave the man who held her son so tenderly, no matter how easy he tried to make the separation.

And she knew deep inside that the longing that gripped her was not only for the sake of her son's heart, but also for her own.

Two days later, back in Michael's house, Suzanne watched as Michael settled Bobby back against his pillow and tenderly adjusted the covers over the boy who'd finally fallen asleep after crying so hard she'd been sick with worry.

Bobby had been too quiet, even through the funeral. She'd tried to get him to talk about his feelings, but he'd insisted he was fine, no matter that she could see the pain spilling out around the edges of his unnatural control.

He'd let her hold him close and he'd seemed to draw comfort from it, but there was a stillness about him that worried her all through the packing and loading up to take him home to Prosperino.

He'd barely touched his dinner and even Maverick could not seem to move him. It was as though he knew that the slightest crack would break him.

Until he'd climbed into bed and accepted her kisses and even then, he'd held himself still. Too still. He'd asked for Michael and something Michael said had finally released the tears. Bobby had cried for a long time in Michael's arms, and she'd stood by, feeling helpless.

Michael leaned over and placed one tender kiss on Bobby's forehead. Then he stood and turned away from her, his shoulders sagging. The one quick glimpse of his face worried her almost as much as she was concerned about her son. But Michael brushed past her and headed quickly down the stairs.

She didn't know what to do for him, didn't know how far to probe. So instead, she gave him his privacy and remained with her son, holding his small hand

and studying his face. Please, she begged. Please let me be enough for him. Let me shield him from further hurt.

After long moments passed and Bobby still slept soundly, exhausted from his tears, she turned her thoughts to Michael, worrying about him, too. Gently she released the small fingers that had fallen slack in hers. She rose and gave Maverick a slow pat where he lay curled up beside his beloved master. "Watch over him," she whispered, "while I check on Michael."

She closed the door quietly and went downstairs, searching everywhere for Michael but finding him nowhere. Finally, she moved to the breakfast room door and saw him sitting outside in the darkness, moonlight gilding his strong frame. He sat on the bench of the picnic table, looking out over the moonlit vista, elbows propped on his knees, chin resting on his clasped hands.

She couldn't decide whether to go to him or leave him alone. He looked so weary. So alone. She realized that he would never ask for comfort, even if he needed it. He'd been a tower of strength for both her and Bobby these last difficult days. He was a tower of strength for his town and his parents, always ready to help whoever needed him.

But who helped Michael? Who let him lean, even for a few precious moments?

No one, she knew instantly. She couldn't think of

a single time she'd ever seen him lean on another soul. He was the tall oak, the mighty sequoia who supported everyone else. He'd been going full-speed for days now, even weeks, as the water crisis kept everyone off balance—and then she and Bobby had complicated the picture.

Even a man as strong as Michael could use a friend, surely. He may not have been willing to let her in further, but he had never tried to stop her from being his friend. If her heart ached for more, that was her problem—but she would not withhold her friendship simply because he wanted no more.

So Suzanne took a deep breath, opened the door to the deck and stepped outside. Fingers fidgeting at her skirt, she crossed toward him. "Michael?"

His shoulders lifted in a weary sigh, but he kept his head averted. "Is it Bobby? Do you need me?"

Yes, she wanted to shout. I need you. Bobby needs you. But he didn't want that. "No," she said softly. "I was worried about you."

His head shook negligently. "I'm fine." But his voice was rougher than usual.

She took a few steps around to his side. "I wanted to thank you. Bobby needed to cry, but he just couldn't seem to let go. I don't know what you said to him, but whatever it was, he needed to hear it. He'll never heal if he doesn't grieve, and he's been unnaturally—"

She stopped in shock. In the moonlight, she saw

the glitter of moisture in Michael's eyes. She didn't know whether to stay or leave.

Just as he'd said she did, she let her heart lead. With three quick steps, she was in front of him. "What is it, Michael?"

Brusquely he shook his head and turned away. His voice was harsh. "Nothing." Then with effort, he softened it. "Just go inside, Suzanne. Please. Give me a minute."

Part of her wanted to obey him, didn't want to embarrass him. But part of her heard the anguish beneath his command.

He looked so alone.

She couldn't leave him. She reached out a trembling hand and stroked his hair. She felt his powerful frame vibrate, but she didn't stop. "Talk to me, Michael. Let me be your friend."

He held himself so still, so stiffly. Then slowly, so slowly she could almost be imagining it, his head sank against her, resting between her breasts as if he could bear his aloneness no more.

Her throat closed up tight, and she closed her eyes against the burn of tears. She opened her hand wide against the back of his head and caressed it, sliding her other arm over his back and cradling him against her.

His arms wrapped around her like steel bands. A shudder wracked his body.

"It's all right, Michael," she crooned. "Let go... just let go for a while."

For a moment this very strong man clung to her, drawing in deep breaths, fighting for control. Waves of pain emanated from him and rolled over her.

Desperate to comfort him, to return some measure of all that he'd given her and her son, she slid to her knees before him and took his face in her hands, kissing first one eyelid and then the other, then seeking out his mouth, only intending to kiss him sweetly, to share with him some part of the strength he'd given her.

But then the kiss changed. Suddenly comfort turned to blazing need. Michael pulled her into his arms and kissed her fiercely, almost desperately, the fire inside him leaping past the flimsy barrier of what she knew was sensible. And she had to answer.

Logic was the first casualty of the blaze that had been smoldering between them from the first. For what seemed like eons, she'd been resisting the potent lure of this man. They'd dodged sparks and thrown water on every tiny flare, but like a brushfire, the hunger between them leapt every barrier they'd erected between what was logical and what their hearts wanted. What their bodies demanded.

Michael lifted her to his lap while his lips burned a path from her mouth down her throat. Nimble fingers opened buttons and dismissed clasps until she was bare to the waist under the stars and the moon.

Then his hot mouth closed over her nipple, and Suzanne's head fell back in surrender. There was no world but Michael, no reality but this man and how much he already meant to her.

With tongue and teeth and hands, he made her wild. He drew a passion from her far beyond anything she'd dreamed. He lifted her as though she weighed nothing and strode inside with her and up the stairs, eyes dark with mingled sorrow and need begging her to join him in holding reality at bay.

In truth, she wanted respite herself this night. For too long she'd walked on eggshells, falling more under his spell each day. He didn't want to love her, he swore he wouldn't love her, and yet she had hope, however foolish, that he would change his mind.

She was already more than half in love with him, foolish or not, hopeless or not. Perhaps there was no way to sway him. Perhaps she would lose. But she knew she was strong enough to handle whatever life cast her way. If Michael never loved her, still he needed her now, needed the surcease the night would bring. Whether or not he would ever admit it, his soul needed rest and it was in her power to give it.

And she needed this night, too, however much pain lay in her future. It would be no worse, surely, to have to leave with this memory to warm her than to leave and always wonder. On long, cold nights in the future she would build for her son, she would treasure this one night, no matter how bittersweet the memory. For

one night she would share herself—all of herself—
with Michael Longstreet.

The best man she'd ever known.

And with that resolve came a quickening of hunger
so deep she felt faint. With shaking fingers, she
reached for Michael's buttons as she lay on his huge
bed with only the moon to light their way.

Suddenly he gripped her hands and stilled them.
"Suzanne, if I could love anyone, it would be you,
but—" His eyes, so hungry and dark and sad, said
the rest.

"Shh." She stopped his words with her fingers,
then replaced the fingers with her kiss. "I know," she
soothed, her heart cracking but resolute. "I understand."

"Do you?" he whispered harshly, holding his body
still, though she felt a quiver arc from his body to
hers.

"Yes." Fiercely she kissed him and concentrated
on his buttons until she could blink back the tears of
grief waiting to snare her. Not now, she ordered herself. I'll grieve later, but not tonight.

Soon they were both naked, and Suzanne saw the
power of the body she'd wondered about so many
times. His body was a warrior's, layered with muscle,
his chest dusted with hair darker than on his head.
His gaze swept over her and his hands followed suit.
Goose bumps rose over her body as he brought the
fire to an inferno.

"You're so small," he murmured. "I don't want to hurt you."

Wild for him as she was, she couldn't repress a shiver. He was big—all over.

His eyes crinkled as her gaze dropped to study him, then they turned serious once again. "We don't have to—"

She stopped his words with a kiss. "Oh yes, we do." Lifting herself to her knees, she paused and lifted her hair in her hands, then let the long locks fall, loving how his eyes darkened, how his body leaped.

With one smooth motion, he rolled to his back and lifted her to straddle him, then reached into the drawer of the nightstand and drew out a foil packet.

Suzanne plucked it from his fingers even as she rocked her hips and felt him buck beneath her as though he'd touched a live wire. He was hard and sleek beneath her and it would take only a slight shift to bring him inside her.

Michael's hands gripped her waist, and a smile broke through like sunlight. "Vixen." He reared up and fastened his mouth on one breast.

It was Suzanne's turn to suck in a deep breath and pray for patience. He felt so good beneath her and around her that she wanted him inside her with a fierceness she'd never known.

Her fingers fumbled and finally she tore at the package with her teeth, cursing beneath her breath.

She could feel Michael chuckle deep in his chest, feel the breath of his laughter over her fevered skin. Never in her life had she laughed while making love, but she might have known nothing with Michael would be like anyone else.

He slid his tongue to the other breast and she wanted to die. "Oh, Michael." Her breath came hard and uneven.

He straightened, his face only inches from hers, lines of need stark on his face. "Suzanne." He shuddered and gripped her more tightly. She'd never felt the power of her femininity more in her life.

She closed her arms around his shoulders, holding the circlet of latex in her hand, and kissed him with all the fervor in her heart. One kiss now before she lost her mind completely. One chance to pour the new love in her heart over whatever was left of his. "I—" I love you, Michael. She bit back the words, knowing they would burden him, not help him. She would tell him with her body the words he did not want to hear, the words she'd promised never to utter.

She broke off the kiss as he went too still beneath her, put on guard by how tightly she held him, perhaps. Pretending a lightness she didn't feel, she pushed him to his back and slid down over his thighs.

When she touched him, he sucked in a gasp. Suzanne smiled wickedly at him and lowered her head, taking him in her mouth.

Michael groaned from his depths and thrust toward

her, then forced her away and sheathed himself. "No, you don't," he warned. "We've waited too long for this."

His hands on her hips, he lifted her and eased her down with a gentleness at odds with the wire-tight tension in his body.

Suzanne let her head fall back and moaned as she took him inside. Then she fell forward against his body, loving the feel of him so full inside her.

Though his body shook with the strain, he stayed still to let her get used to him. "Are you all right?" he whispered.

She lifted her head and smiled slowly, licking her lips. "Oh yeah." And to prove her point, she rocked her hips and seated him to the hilt.

Then no more thought was possible, no more words could be uttered, no more caution could exist. It was all heat and hunger and fierce, driving need. With fingers and lips and the driving beat of his hard body, Michael made her his, imprinted himself forever on every part of her. He rendered her all but senseless with the skill and care he gave to sending her soaring even as she felt how close he was to exploding.

Suddenly she wanted to be under him, to know the full possession of this man, to revel in his power and his command, to feel all woman to this very potent man. She leaned to the side as she fastened her mouth to his throat, and he responded quickly, rolling them and bringing her under him, towering over her like every hero she'd ever read in the novels that couldn't touch the reality of this man.

"Michael," she pleaded, spinning out toward unknown reaches as her fingers dug into his skin, her own flesh ready to burst from the power of the hunger that drove them on, made them one.

"Come with me, Suzanne," he urged. "Look at me. Let me see those beautiful eyes. Know that it's me, Suzanne," and his voice went husky. "Know that it's me."

She opened her eyes and feasted on what she saw there, what she felt shimmer in the air around them. "You, Michael. Only you." She ached from the longing to tell him the words. I love you.

They were there in his eyes, closer to the surface than she'd ever dreamed, but suddenly grief, sharp as a knife, pierced through. He broke the gaze too quickly, dipping his head to hers in a kiss that she knew was designed to distract her from the knowledge that even now when they were as close as breath and bone, his heart was not his own. For a moment she wanted to grieve herself, but there would be time for that later. Right now every nerve in her body wanted this moment, this man, this wildfire between them.

His kiss sent her over, sent her spinning, sent her far beyond herself so that she barely heard the deep, powerful groan as Michael joined her in bliss, exploding against her, then collapsing in her arms, a welcome weight that she would concentrate on to block out the knowledge that had settled into her heart.

It was the finest lovemaking she'd ever known. He was the man of her dreams. Life with him would be magic; it would be everything she'd ever wanted.

Except for one thing.

Even at the moment that her heart was his and she knew his heart wanted hers—even then, when ecstasy claimed them and they had everything within their grasp, when they could have moved mountains, when she would have sold her soul to stay with him—a dead woman and her child still had first claim.

She should have resented it, should have been furious. Should have left his bed and walked out of his life.

Instead, Suzanne ached for this man whose sense of honor required him to forego what he needed most. And she couldn't find it in her heart to resent him when she would have given anything to have someone love her that much.

So she wrapped her arms around the man who wouldn't let himself accept her love and held him close, even as her heart broke.

# Eleven

As dawn crept into the room, Michael studied every curve of her body, every line of her face as Suzanne lay snuggled against him. The trust she displayed while sleeping beside him raked his heart over the coals because he did not deserve that trust.

Across the hall he heard Bobby whimper and rose from the bed quietly, covering Suzanne's beautiful body carefully, then slipped on his pants silently and stole from the room.

When he opened Bobby's door, Maverick raised his head and thumped his tail softly. With a touch, Michael quieted him and stood over the sleeping child. When Bobby slept on peacefully, Michael turned to go downstairs, his heart heavy.

In one night, in the space of a few hours, he'd betrayed Elaine. Betrayed his child. Despite all he'd thought of his honor, he'd let first a lonely boy into his heart, and then the boy's mother, despite a solemn vow over a grave.

Even less forgivable, he'd felt things with Suzanne that he'd never felt before in his life. What had passed between them had been so sweet and so hot, so all-consuming that he'd lost sight of all else, had even gone so far as to forget, for those moments, the woman and child he'd promised to love forever.

What he'd felt for Suzanne stunned him. For countless moments, she'd been everything—all he could see, all he could hear, all he could want. When he'd realized he'd never felt this bliss, the connection to Elaine had shivered like a spiderweb before a broom—and the ecstasy of Suzanne had turned to bitter ashes on his tongue.

How could he possibly have felt more for Suzanne than for Elaine, whom he had loved? Elaine was his heart, his life, and he'd failed her so badly in his selfish desire to show his parents that he could have it all without them.

He had no heart to give Suzanne, no love to give her son. Both were buried in Connecticut, never to rise again.

It had been wrong, so very wrong to yield to the comfort Suzanne offered from her generous heart. A thousand images from the night raced through his brain. Suzanne holding him against her, comforting without words. Suzanne laughing with breathtaking mischief in her eyes. Suzanne, pale as a moonbeam and lovely enough to stun. If he lived to be a hundred, he would never forget the night they just passed.

But it could never happen again. He would be more careful, that was all. He'd never lose control again like that.

No matter how much he ached for a woman he could not have.

The phone rang, slicing into his thoughts. He frowned, glancing at the clock. Six a.m. "Hello?"

"Mr. Mayor," said the voice of the city utility director. "You'd better get down here quick. We've registered DMBE in the city wells."

Michael's mind recoiled. Quickly he recovered. "I'll be there in thirty minutes."

He hung up the phone and headed upstairs to shower and then wake Suzanne.


"Suzanne," said the voice from her dreams.

She stirred faintly, then sighed and smiled. Michael. For a precious second, all she could remember was utter bliss.

"Suzanne." The urgency in his voice sank in.

She opened her eyes to see Michael leaning over her, his green eyes dark with worry and something deeper. She sat up. "What's wrong? Is it Bobby?"

"No. Bobby's fine. He's still asleep. It's early."

His hair was damp, and he wore a new set of clothes. Finally it registered that he had on a coat and was ready to go.

He stepped away from her, his eyes carefully distant.

"What is it?" Bliss vanished like the mist. In its place, cold dread grew. At last she remembered the moment when they should have been rapturous; instead, he'd grieved.

"I have to go to town." His face was so solemn.

"Is everything—" Suddenly she knew. "Oh, no. The wells."

He nodded. "They just registered it in the first well."

"What does that mean, Michael? What will we do?"

"I can't tell you yet. Joe's people are out of time. We need a solution."

She was already scrambling from the bed when she realized she had no robe. She looked around for something to put on and grabbed his shirt from the floor before she saw his gaze flicker.

Like a hot potato, she dropped it and wrapped the sheet around her body, feeling too vulnerable to him. Mustering all the aplomb she could gather, she smoothed back her hair, gripping it in an impromptu ponytail. "I'll fix you some breakfast."

He shook his head quickly. "No time. I have to

go. I just—'' He glanced toward her. "I didn't want to leave without—"

A thousand unspoken words floated in the air between them, the weight of each one hanging heavier on her heart with each second that passed.

"Suzanne, when I come back, we need to talk." As grim as his voice was, she could take no comfort. His regret pelted her soul like a shower of sharp stones.

She had no response. What could she say? Love me and not your dead wife? How could you make love to me like that when you're still tied to her? Every thought that winged her way was loaded with either blame or plea, and she would not burden him with either.

He'd never lied to her. He'd made the ground rules clear. She couldn't cry foul like some innocent maiden. She'd known he didn't want to love her, known he was giving as much as he had to give.

But she'd hoped. After the glory of their joining, after she'd felt her soul wing its way to his, she'd foolishly and blindly hoped that he would change his mind.

But he hadn't lied. And torment rode every line of his face now. It would be selfish in the extreme to chastise him for being true to exactly what he'd offered.

"Go ahead," she ground out. Lifting her gaze, she

tried to send him off with a smile, but the look on his face would have told her she'd failed even if she couldn't feel the crack in her heart.

He started to turn but hesitated. "Will you be all right?" he asked in a low voice.

Oh, God. Why couldn't he be a jerk so she could hate him? She swallowed hard and worked on that smile. "I'll be fine. You go do what you have to do."

He nodded and turned, his tread heavy as he moved toward the door. He didn't turn back as he spoke. "I'll have my cell phone if you need me. We should have enough bottled water for a few days, and the well for this house is far enough away that it should be safe, but I'm taking a sample with me to get it tested again."

She smiled. Ever the protector. "We'll be careful. And thank you." Thank you for the bliss. Thank you for being so generous. Now if only you could open up that stupid rusty heart...

He nodded again and opened the door.

"Michael?"

He stopped. "Yes?"

Fear gripped her. The more time that elapsed, the more distant he grew. Soon they would only be polite strangers, and she grieved already for the loss.

But she couldn't make this harder on him than it already was. "Just be careful, okay?"

With one more nod, he was gone.

Suzanne sank to the bed and stared sightlessly at a view that, on any other day, would have been stunning.

Michael called that night, his voice heavy. "I still can't believe it. David Corbett arrested and charged."

"The vice president at Springer? With what?"

"Disregard for human life and attempted murder." Michael paused. "He swears he's innocent."

Suzanne felt chilled. "He's helped me with fundraising for Emily's House."

"I know. I've worked with him several times on issues affecting Springer and Prosperino. He just—he doesn't seem like someone who would do something like that." They were both silent, thinking. Then he spoke again. "Todd Lamb is his replacement. He's Holly's father."

"Blake's secretary Holly?"

"Yeah." Exhaustion rippled through his tone.

No matter how awkward things had been left between them, she couldn't help responding. "Come home, Michael. You need to rest."

"I can't. Not yet. How's Bobby?"

"He's subdued. I kept him busy today. He wants to know when you're coming home."

A long silence ensued. "Suzanne..."

She wanted to scream. Wanted to beg. Wanted to turn back the clock to last night.

His voice turned neutral. "I'll do the best I can. Tell him good night for me." Then he was gone.

As she put Bobby to bed, she noticed how pale and listless he was, perhaps more than before. She couldn't tell if it was sorrow or illness. She was used to pushing herself and wondered if she'd kept up too strong a pace for Bobby, too.

She brushed his hair off his forehead and kissed him to check his temperature, but he didn't feel warm. "You okay, Bobby Bear?" she asked.

He smiled up at her. "Yeah. Just kinda tired."

"We did a lot today, didn't we?" She'd decided it was too soon to start him in his new school. Next week would be soon enough. So she'd taken him with her to the Colton ranch to check on her kids, and everyone there had treated him like a mascot. While some of the boys showed him around, she'd thanked Blake again for letting her have time off to get Bobby settled. Blake knew the situation and had been sworn to silence. Until Bobby knew she was his mother, they would stick to the cover story that he was simply a friend's child for whom she and Michael were caring.

"When's Michael coming home?" Bobby asked.

She sighed. "I don't know. When he called, he still had reporters to talk to and more plans to work out."

"He's really important, isn't he?" There was pride there.

She nodded. "Yes. Right now he's especially important because people are looking to him to lead them."

"Because the water's bad?" Bobby asked.

She hadn't tried to hide the danger. Bobby needed to know to be careful what he consumed until the crisis was over.

"Yes. People are afraid, but Michael says that Mr. Colton's experts have figured out a way to treat the water, so he's hoping the citizens will calm down once word gets around." She smiled. "But we still need to be really careful until Michael says it's clear, even though our well tested out all right."

Bobby nodded, then did one of those lightning-fast changes of subject that children did. "I liked the kids where you work. They were pretty cool to me." He grinned. "Some of the boys say you're the ench."

Suzanne stifled a groan. She wasn't ready for teen-speak from Bobby. Then she grinned and gently tapped his nose. "And what do you think?"

"I think my dad was right." Sorrow drifted over his sweet face. "He said you would do everything you could to make it not hurt so much."

"Oh, sweetie…" She gathered him into her arms. "I wish I could make it all go away right this second, but it's just what happens when we lose someone we love. It's part of love, but it will get better after a while."

"I don't want to forget my dad, Suzanne," he whispered.

"I don't want you to forget him either. He was a very good man, the best kind of man."

Bobby leaned his head back. "Like Michael."

An ache speared through her, but she nodded. "That's right. Just like Michael."

"What's like Michael?" a deep voice asked.

Both she and Bobby jumped, then Bobby wriggled from her arms and raced from the bed. "Michael!" he shouted, leaping into the man's arms.

Suzanne cringed as she saw the pain on Michael's face, but he didn't rebuff her son. Instead, he engaged in a few moments of horseplay until Bobby collapsed in giggles.

Michael looked exhausted, so gently she urged Bobby back to bed, but nothing would do but that Michael tuck him in.

She started to intervene, but Michael shook his head. Instead, he talked quietly with Bobby, helping him calm down and get ready for sleep. Bobby's small hand slipped trustingly into his, and Suzanne ached for both of them.

She stepped back toward the door when Bobby spoke in a sleepy voice.

"Michael, sometimes I wish you would be my new dad. Would my dad be upset that I wish it?"

She saw raw anguish slide over Michael's face, and she knew in that moment that they'd made a terrible mistake. They'd underestimated the price on Bobby of their marriage of convenience. Every one of them would suffer—but none more than this innocent child.

She didn't stay to hear his answer. She couldn't

listen. All she could think was that it was over, that there was no way she could stay one second longer and let Bobby get more and more attached to a man no sane person could resist.

The knowledge left her trembling with fury—blind, raging fury at whom, she wasn't sure. Herself, certainly, for being so naive. Michael, for clinging to a love long dead when he could have one that lived. And fate, the coldhearted witch, for taking Jim Roper from the son who needed him so much.

When Michael walked out of Bobby's room, they faced each other in profound silence, the knowledge as plain on his face as it must be on hers that the stakes had changed.

"Let's talk downstairs," he said grimly, though he looked ready to fall on the floor in exhaustion.

"Fine." This couldn't wait.

When they reached the kitchen, she tried desperately to hold on to the fury that simmered.

"Suzanne—"

"I'm leaving. Tomorrow. Bobby and I will be out of here as soon as I can pack."

"What?" He looked at her, stunned. "Why?"

"Why?" It was a match to tinder. "After that, you can ask me why? He's getting too attached, and you have no intention of loving him back."

"I didn't say—"

"You don't have to say a word." Fury dug in its spurs. "You made it abundantly obvious last night that your heart is dead and gone.'' When he started to speak, she held up a hand. ''You warned me, I know. But like a stupid fool, I fell in love with you, even knowing I'm not your type of woman.''

''What do you mean, you fell—''

She rode right over his words. ''But I'm not the issue here. I'll get over it, but I won't let you break my son's heart, too.'' She glared as fire shot through her veins. ''I want you to tell me what's wrong with my son that he's not good enough to gain your love. You tell me where that boy falls short because from here, he seems like one very wonderful kid.''

''He is a wonderful kid. He's the best. If I could love any child, I'd love him.''

She shoved away the hurt of being excluded from that statement. ''Why, Michael? Why can't you love him?'' Why can't you love me?

His voice was soft but fierce. ''I made a promise.''

''To whom?''

''To them. To Elaine and the baby.''

''What kind of promise?''

''That I'd never replace them.'' And the depths of his grief and guilt dug deep grooves in his face. ''They're dead because of me, and I owe them that, at least.''

''Why do you say it's because of you?''

''She'd told me the day before that there was something strange about the brakes, but we couldn't afford a mechanic and I was too rushed to check them that day, too worried about school and my job and proving to my folks that they were wrong about me. We argued that morning because she'd tried to call my parents behind my back to make peace, but they weren't home. We had a terrible fight. She left, and I never saw her alive again. Her brakes failed, and she was hit in a major intersection. The baby died with her.''

God. How horrible for him.

''I can't be alive when they're not, don't you understand? Elaine taught me how to love, how to take joy from every day. She taught me everything I know about what's meaningful in life and how to make it count. I can't betray that like I did last night when you and I—'' He fell silent.

''Say it, Michael. When we made love. Because that's what it was. It wasn't sex. It wasn't about using someone's body. Until you let your guilt creep in, we were as close as two people ever get to be.'' She leaned toward him. ''Your heart touched my heart, Michael, can't you see that?''

''You don't understand.'' His jaw hardened.

She looked at him for a moment, all her rage falling away and replaced by the weariness of knowing that he would never let go of his grief. But she had to make one last stab, though it would hurt them both.

''Elaine would be ashamed of you.''

Fire sparked in his eyes. ''What the hell does that mean?''

''You say she taught you to love, and look at what

you're doing. You're acting like love's a sin, when it's right there in front of you for the taking. You want it as badly as I do, but you won't break some vow that Elaine never asked you to make.'' She saw rage in his features, but she went on, anyway. ''The circumstances just before she died were terrible and tragic, but the woman you described to me would consider it a far greater sin to cast away love when it's offered to you. That woman would never have intended you to spend the rest of your life with your heart locked away in mourning. She would have told you to live and honor what she taught you, to honor her love by giving it to others.''

His voice was a low growl. ''You don't know what she was like, how she could light up a room, how she lived in that rat-trap for my sake, how she stayed at that nothing job for me.'' He jabbed a thumb into his own chest. ''For me, for love of me, she lived with even less than she'd had before me so that I could go on with my dreams while hers were put on hold. It's pretty damn poor repayment that my stubborn pride cost her life, wouldn't you say?'' The anguish in his face hurt Suzanne so badly that she wanted to stop this now, but she knew she was hearing things he'd never told anyone else.

''It was all I had to give her,'' he whispered. ''My heart. My damn worthless heart that demanded too much of her. That dazzled her with dreams she'd never get to share.'' His voice broke. ''She wanted a big old two-story house like this, you know that? She wanted to fill it with children. Our children. Simple dreams she should have been able to have. Instead she had nothing.''

"She had a dream I'd sell my soul to have, Michael," Suzanne whispered. "She had you. All of you." Blinded by tears, by the agony of knowing that she would never have his love, all Suzanne wanted was to get away, to lick her wounds in private. She turned to go.

He caught her arm. "Suzanne, I—"

She couldn't look back. She pulled away, but at that moment she heard Bobby scream in fear and pain.

Whatever Michael meant to say would have to wait as they raced up the stairs.

When they burst into his room, Bobby was writhing in pain and he'd vomited all over the bed.

"Oh, God," Suzanne moaned. "That's what happened with the kids at the ranch."

"What did he drink? Where did you go today?" Michael asked, but he was already scooping Bobby up into his arms.

"I don't know. We went to the Coltons' ranch, and we stopped in town, but I never saw him drink anything, and he knew better than to—"

"Come on. It would take too long to get an ambulance up here. We'll drive him into town. You ride in the back with him."

Swiftly they made their way out to the car, Bobby holding his stomach and crying out in agony. Suzanne's heart beat a tattoo as she tried to think what could have happened

Michael drove swiftly but surely and soon, they were racing into the emergency room, Michael's long strides covering ground with Bobby in his arms while she answered rapid-fire questions from the staff.

# Twelve

"Michael." The door to the examining room opened, and Blake Fallon walked in with a man Michael didn't know. Michael stopped pacing, but all he could think about was his fear for Bobby and his concern for Suzanne, who stood beside the bed stroking Bobby's head as he slept uneasily while they waited for the results of all the tests.

Blake crossed the room and spoke to Suzanne briefly, hugging her as Michael would like to do. But his ears still rang with their bitter words in the kitchen, and he knew he was probably the last person Suzanne wanted nearby.

Then Blake stood in front of him. "Can we talk outside?"

Michael frowned and glanced at Suzanne, but she'd already turned back to her child. "Sure. But I don't want to go far."

"I understand," Blake said.

Once they were outside, he introduced the other man. "Mayor Michael Longstreet, this is a friend of mine, Rafe James. He's a private investigator."

Michael studied the other man as they shook hands. Then he turned to Blake. "So what are you doing here?"

Blake smiled faintly. "Rafe was in my office visiting me when I got word that one of the Hopechest kids had gotten hurt out at the Coltons' and needed stitches, so I told them I'd meet them here." He shook his head ruefully. "Kids." Then he seemed to remember why Michael was here. "I'm sorry. You must be worried sick."

He shouldn't be, but he was. His careful distance from Bobby had never materialized. "Suzanne's the one who's having the worst of it." He couldn't tell Blake that Bobby was her natural child, but he could see the questions in Blake's eyes. "My well tested fine. I don't know where he could have gotten the water, but—" He broke off, furious at his inability to get this damn water situation resolved. "Any more word on Corbett? Is he still claiming ignorance?"

Rafe James spoke up. "Something's not right here. I know David Corbett. He isn't capable of something like this. He's a good man."

Michael nodded. "That was always my read on him, too. But the FBI seems to think differently."

James nodded. "Corbett's daughter Libby is an attorney in San Francisco. She's flying in to take over his case, but I told Blake I'm going to hang around, do my own investigation. Something just doesn't smell right."

"Nothing's been right around this town for weeks." Michael felt the weight of all the days and weeks of tension. Suddenly he was as tired as he'd ever been in his life.

"It's been a long haul, buddy." Blake clapped him on the shoulder. "You want us to wait here with you?"

Michael shook his head. "No. We'll be fine." How he hoped that was true. If anything happened to that boy—

But he couldn't think that way. Even if she didn't want him near, Suzanne needed him to stay strong to help her fight her own fears.

He shook Rafe James's hand. "Good luck. Let me know if I can help with anything."

The other man nodded. "I will."

Michael turned to Blake. "And you, my friend, don't look a lot better than I feel. Go hit the sack."

"I think I will. But you call if you two need anything, all right?"

"Will do." Michael waved them off and went back into the room.

Suzanne stood watching her son sleep, arms wrapped around her slender waist, her body bowed inward beneath the weight of her fear. He wanted to go to her, wanted to hold her—but after the angry words they'd exchanged, he had no right.

He rubbed his eyes. God, he was tired. So tired he was making mistakes, losing his judgment. He didn't know how Bobby had gotten hold of contaminated water, but he should never have let Suzanne bring the boy back here in the first place. It didn't matter that the house had been so empty without her that he'd jumped at the chance to bring them home after the funeral. He should have sent them away somewhere, anywhere they'd be safe. If anything happened to Bobby or to Suzanne...

Something deep inside him shuddered. He couldn't lose them. He couldn't go through that again. But when Suzanne had said they were leaving, all he could think was that he had to make her stay, had to find a way to keep her near.

And suddenly he knew. Suzanne had it right, but only part of it. When she'd said Elaine would be ashamed of him, that he did Elaine's love no honor, he'd lashed out with words because she'd struck at the heart of something he'd buried beneath the weight of his vow never to replace them.

But he knew now that it was fear that kept him frozen in grief—fear of ever knowing that pain again, ever putting his heart in harm's way by loving anyone

as much as he'd loved Elaine. As much as he'd
wanted their child.

And when he'd realized that what he felt for Suzanne was many times stronger than anything he'd
shared even with Elaine, it struck right at the core of
him, dead center of his guilt. He'd known in that moment of ecstasy that what he and Suzanne could have
would be more powerful than anything he'd ever
dreamed.

And it scared him to death. Because he didn't know
if he could survive it if anything happened to Suzanne. He knew only too well how puny man's powers were against the hand of fate.

But now he looked across the stark, sterile room at
a boy he loved against reason, at a small woman with
the heart of a lion, a woman who fought with everything in her for those who needed her.

Could he do less? How long would he let the pain
win? When everything he wanted was right here
within his grasp, what was he waiting for?

So he crossed the floor to offer himself to a woman
who might no longer want him. But he had to try.

"Suzanne," he said softly, one hand hovering over
her delicate shoulder.

She turned toward him, her eyes huge with her terror, but she didn't speak.

He didn't know where to start. "I told the staff to
spare no expense. I've asked them to bring in spe-
cialists or we'll fly Bobby to San Francisco if needed.

Anything, Suzanne. Anything I have is yours. I—''
He took a deep breath. ''I care about that boy. I want
him well and safe.''

If anything, her eyes darkened with pain. For a moment she closed her eyes as though unable to look at
him.

He wanted to touch her so badly he ached, but he'd
hurt her too much already. She had to be the one to
let him in.

With effort, she straightened and looked right at
him. ''Thank you, Michael. I don't know how I'll
repay you, but somehow I will.''

''Suzanne, don't—'' His own pain bled through in
his voice. ''It's not about money. I love Bobby.''

Her head jerked up and for a moment, he expected
sparks. Instead, he saw defeat. ''That will only make
it harder when we leave,'' she whispered.

He knew in that second that he would never let her
leave of his own volition. But he had work to do to
convince her, and he wasn't sure how she felt about
him now. There was nothing of the fiery angel in the
woman before him, nothing of the woman who led
with her heart. She was still, too still.

He couldn't find the right starting place, so he just
took a deep breath and leapt in. ''Don't leave, Suzanne. Please. You were right. I do no honor to
Elaine's memory by burying myself with her. She
would hate that. I just…I felt so helpless. I felt so
responsible, and I didn't know how to make it right.''

"Michael." She touched his arm with her hand, and he wanted to shout out his hope. Her violet eyes were soft now, but he had to be sure it wasn't pity.

"Don't feel sorry for me. Look what I've done to you and to Bobby. I don't—" He looked away, desperate to find the words. Then he snapped his gaze back to hers. "You make me feel too much, Suzanne. You make me want you so much. I don't know how to handle it. I couldn't—" He swallowed hard. "I couldn't stand it if something happened to you, too. And now there's Bobby, and I love that boy like my own, and you want to leave and—"

Her hand rose and touched his cheek, her eyes shimmering with tears. "You mean—" The tears spilled over. "What are you saying, Michael?"

He grasped her hand in his and tangled their fingers together, never wanting to let her go. "I'm saying that I love you, that I've never loved anyone the way I love you. That I want you and I want Bobby, that I want us to build a life together. But I'm so damned afraid of losing you." He brought her fingers to his lips. "God, I don't want to be this vulnerable again, Suzanne. I fought it and threw my vow to Elaine up between us, trying so damn hard not to love you."

Suzanne smiled through the tears rolling down her cheeks. "But you do, anyway?" All the hope and love in the world lay shimmering in a violet mist.

He smiled back and stroked his thumb across her cheek, catching her tears. "Heaven help me, I do."

He leaned closer. "More than I've ever loved anyone, Suzanne. So much I don't know what to do with all of it."

"Give it to me," she whispered, rising to her toes and pressing a soft kiss on his lips. "Give it to me and to Bobby. We can build a life on that love, Michael."

He wanted to draw her against him, but first he had to know. "What about you? Can you love me?"

"Oh, Michael. I think I lost my heart with that first kiss in Ruby's, and I've been trying ever since to get it back."

"Finders keepers," he whispered. "I'll give you anything you want, if you'll just let me keep your heart. If you'll trust me with it." He swallowed hard. "I don't know if it's smart, though, Suzanne. Maybe you want to be careful, see how things go."

She smiled and for a moment, it was like sunshine in this dark night. "But you said it yourself, Mr. Mayor. I'm never careful and I always lead with my heart." She slid her free hand around his neck and drew him close.

Michael abandoned all caution and pulled her tightly into his arms, lowering his mouth to hers. "Don't ever change, Suzanne. Teach me your way." And then they were there, right back in the magic again, only this time it was deeper and richer for the knowledge that love lived inside them, that love would light their way.

Michael was so deep into the spell Suzanne cast, so grateful to find a home in her love, that he didn't hear the sound behind them at first. It registered on both of them at the same moment, the clearing of a throat behind them.

When Suzanne leapt away from him, he saw guilt ride her hard and knew it himself, that even for a second they could let go of the fear for the boy they both loved.

But the nurse and Dr. Jason Colton were smiling, and Michael's guilt eased. He wrapped an arm around Suzanne and followed Jason's gesture, joining him in the hallway while the nurse kept watch inside. "What's wrong with Bobby?"

"It's not the water," Jason said.

Michael felt Suzanne's slight frame relax and drew her closer. "What is it?"

"His appendix, but you got him here in time. We'll need to take him up to surgery in a few minutes. Come with me while I explain to him what's going to happen."

Suzanne was off like a shot, and Michael was close behind her. Jason leaned over the bed where Bobby lay, looking very small and sleepy, groggy from having been awakened. He explained to the boy carefully what would happen, while Michael and Suzanne each held one of Bobby's hands.

Then it was time for Bobby to go. Suzanne leaned over and hugged and kissed him, her tears flowing once again. But she straightened immediately, and Michael could see her arming herself not to frighten him. "I love you, Bobby. Dr. Colton says you're going to be just fine."

Michael looked at the face of the child who'd burrowed deep in his heart, and he smiled. "You scared us, son, but everything's going to be just fine now." He grasped one small hand in his and squeezed. "I love you, Bobby."

Bobby's grin widened. "You called me son."

He nodded. "When you come back, we're going to talk to you about becoming a family, the three of us. Suzanne and I want to adopt you. It was your dad's wish, and I'd be proud to have you as my son. Would you be willing to have Suzanne as your mom and me as your new father? You and Maverick and us, we'd make a new family, if you'd like."

Bobby's eyes darkened a bit as memory flitted past.

Michael was quick to reassure him. "Not to replace your dad, though. No one could do that. But we'd like to be there for you, since Jim can't."

Bobby studied him solemnly. "What would I call you?"

"Whatever you'd like, son."

"I called my father Dad, so maybe I could call you Daddy. Would that be all right?" He glanced at Suzanne. "Think that would be okay...Mom?"

Michael felt a surge run through Suzanne's body like a lightning bolt and knew that was the first time her son had ever called her mom. Suzanne's tears trickled down her face, but Michael saw a huge smile on her face. "I think it would be just wonderful, sweetheart."

Bobby looked at Michael.

Michael nodded, surprised at a thickness in his own throat. "I'd like that, son. Now you go with these good folks and when you wake up again, we'll be right there to take you home." He smiled. "Maverick needs his playmate back. And we need our boy." He squeezed Suzanne against him, then leaned down to kiss Bobby's forehead. "Sleep now, and don't worry about your mom. I'll take care of her."

He watched while Suzanne kissed Bobby again and knew that one day soon, when Bobby's heart had had time to heal from the loss of Jim Roper, they would tell the boy together that he was not only the child of their heart but the child of Suzanne's body.

"'Night, Mom. 'Night, Daddy," Bobby murmured as they wheeled him away.

"Sleep well, sweet child of mine," Suzanne whispered. Then she looked up at Michael, violet eyes soft and filled with wonder. "Oh, Michael…"

Michael took her into his arms and held her close. "Want another wedding, Suzanne? A real one with a white dress and blossoms, like every girl's dream?"

She lifted her face to his, her breath soft against his throat. She held her hand to the light and studied the sparkle of amethysts and diamonds. "I had my violets," she murmured. "But I wouldn't mind having a honeymoon, once Bobby's had time to settle in.''

''Anywhere you want to go, just name it. Paris, the Taj Mahal, Tahiti?''

Suzanne shook her head and smiled. ''I know a place a lot closer. It has this big heart-shaped whirlpool and this thirty-channel remote control sound sys—''

Michael burst out laughing. ''You want to go back to the Jungle Suite?''

Suzanne's eyes sparkled with mischief. ''We never did get to try out all those mirrors.''

Michael grinned and thought about living out every fantasy that room had inspired. Thought about years ahead to watch a son grow and, God willing, to father Suzanne's babies. To grow old in the sunshine of this woman's love when he'd expected to live out his life alone.

He covered her mouth with his and wrapped her tightly in his arms, vowing to make the most of every second fate granted him with this remarkable woman, so much his opposite and so very perfect.

He whispered good-bye to Elaine and their baby, feeling a new and blessed peace settle over his heart as he finally let go of the grief and pain that had been his constant companions for so very long.

And he thanked his lucky stars that sometimes in life, despite what you deserved, you got second chances. He would make this one count.

\* \* \* \* \*

*Don't miss the next installment
of the Colton family saga
with Donna Clayton's*
**CLOSE PROXIMITY.**

*Here's a preview!*

# One

---

**D**avid Corbett had been her champion when she'd been a little girl. Her knight in shining armor. He'd sacrificed so much for her. He'd made her feel secure. He'd made her feel loved. At a time when the awful stammer she suffered made her feel flawed and awkward and often stupid.

Years ago, Libby had been strong for her mother through those long months of her illness. It had about killed her to keep her chin up and a smile on her face, but she'd been proud to offer a shoulder for her mom to lean on. Now the time had arrived for her to be strong for her father. Now was her opportunity to repay him for his years of total devotion and sacrifice.

When her father had called her to request that she
find him a good lawyer, Libby hadn't a clue why he
might need representation. She'd assured him that she
could take care of any personal legal matters he might
have. She might be a criminal attorney, she
remembered telling him, but someone in her firm
could certainly see that his will was properly filed.

Her knees had grown wobbly when he'd finally
confessed that he was calling her from jail, and that
he was facing felony charges.

Disregard for human life? Attempted murder?

That very evening, the story had hit the west coast
newspapers.

How could anyone, the EPA, the FBI and least of
all the executives at Springer, Inc., believe that
straightlaced David Corbett could be guilty of those
crimes?

Libby had immediately gone to the partners in the
firm. She'd requested time away from the practice in
order to give her father the best representation
available. No one had a greater stake in this than she
did. No other attorney would be willing to go to any
lengths to prove her father's innocence like she
would. Together, she and her father would beat this
thing.

Uncertainty, gray and thick, gathered around her
like a wintry coastal mist.

Why had her father balked initially when she'd
proposed she travel north to act as his lawyer? She

hadn't really thought about it at the time, so caught up was she in his plight. Why had he tried so hard to decline her offer of help? Sure, he'd used the excuse of not wanting her life interrupted by what was sure to be a mess—the biggest three-ring circus in the history of Prosperino, he'd said. He'd tried to reason that her professional reputation might be in jeopardy just by having her name associated with the case. However, she couldn't help but wonder if, just maybe, her father doubted her ability as an attorney. Maybe he thought she didn't have the skills necessary to successfully clear his name.

"But I can help you, Daddy," she whispered in the solitude of the car, wretched emotion burning her throat, unshed tears prickling the backs of her eyelids.

Fear gripped her belly with icy fingers when she thought of all the hostility she'd faced at the courthouse today. From the media. From the townspeople. Everyone seemed so dead-set against her dad. Everyone.

Suddenly, she remembered the rich, mahogany eyes of the man who had come to her aid this morning. Never in her life had she experienced an expression filled with such complex and concentrated intensity. The memory made her shiver.

When the man had touched her, when he'd taken her by the arm, the chaos in her mind calmed. She'd felt safe. Secure. He'd been like a haven in the midst of a terrible storm.

But that was silly. Safe and secure with a complete stranger? Come on, Libby, her brain lectured. You're letting down your guard.

That protected feeling had simply come from the fact that he seemed to be on her side when no one else had been. The man must know her father. Must have had some dealings with him. The thought brought her comfort.

Maybe everyone wasn't against her father.

She swallowed. Inhaled deeply. Tipped up her chin. She sure wouldn't be able to clear her father's name by wallowing in doubt and self-pity.

The car key was cool against her palm as she pulled it from the ignition. Shoving open the door, she exited the car, bringing with her the bag of groceries she'd purchased this afternoon and her attaché case. With a small thrust of her hip, she closed the car door. The heels of her shoes clicked on the paved drive as she made her way to the porch.

Libby looked up, and was truly astonished to see him standing on the front lawn. The man with those intense, dark eyes.

LEGACIES . LIES . LOVE .

In February,
RITA® Award-winning author

# KRISTIN GABRIEL

**brings you a brand-new
Forrester Square tale…**

## THIRD TIME'S THE CHARM

Dana Ulrich's wedding planning business
seemed doomed and the next nuptials were
make or break. So Dana turned to best man
Austin Hawke for help. But if Austin had
his way, it would be Dana walking down
the aisle…toward him!

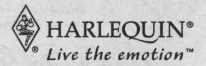

# HARLEQUIN®
*Live the emotion*™

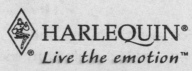